A Christmas Journey

*Also by Anne Perry
in Large Print:*

Funeral in Blue
The Whitechapel Conspiracy
Death of a Stranger
No Graves as Yet
Seven Dials
Southampton Row
Tathea

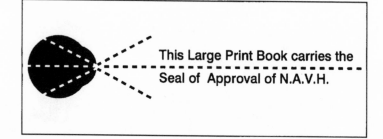

This Large Print Book carries the
Seal of Approval of N.A.V.H.

A Christmas Journey

Anne Perry

Thorndike Press • Waterville, Maine

Published in 2004 by arrangement with The Ballantine Publishing Group, a division of Random House, Inc.

Thorndike Press® Large Print Basic.

The tree indicium is a trademark of Thorndike Press.

The text of this Large Print edition is unabridged.
Other aspects of the book may vary from the original edition.

Set in 16 pt. Plantin by Minnie B. Raven.

Printed in the United States on permanent paper.

Library of Congress Control Number: 2004107818
ISBN 0-7862-6881-6 (lg. print : hc : alk. paper)

To all those who
contribute to the gift of friendship

As the Founder/CEO of NAVH, the only national health agency solely devoted to those who, although not totally blind, have an eye disease which could lead to serious visual impairment, I am pleased to recognize Thorndike Press★ as one of the leading publishers in the large print field.

Founded in 1954 in San Francisco to prepare large print textbooks for partially seeing children, NAVH became the pioneer and standard setting agency in the preparation of large type.

Today, those publishers who meet our standards carry the prestigious "Seal of Approval" indicating high quality large print. We are delighted that Thorndike Press is one of the publishers whose titles meet these standards. We are also pleased to recognize the significant contribution Thorndike Press is making in this important and growing field.

Lorraine H. Marchi, L.H.D.
Founder/CEO
NAVH

★ Thorndike Press encompasses the following imprints: Thorndike, Wheeler, Walker and Large Print Press.

Part One

Lady Vespasia Cumming-Gould hesitated a moment at the top of the stairs. Applecross was one of those magnificent country houses where one descended down a long curved sweep of marble into the vast hall where the assembled guests were gathered awaiting the call to dinner.

First one person, then another looked up. To wait for them all would have been ostentatious. She was dressed in oyster satin, not a shade everyone could wear, but Prince Albert himself had said that she was the most beautiful woman in Europe, with her glorious hair and exquisite bones. It was not a remark that had endeared her to the queen, the more so since it was probably true.

But this was not a royal occasion; it was a simple weekend party early in December. The London season was over with its hectic social round, and those who had country homes had returned to them to look forward to Christmas. There were rumors of possible war in the Crimea, but apart from that the middle of the century saw only greater progress and prosperity within an empire that spanned the globe.

Omegus Jones came to the foot of the stairs to meet her. He was not only the perfect host, but also a friend of some years, even though he was in his fifties and Vespasia barely past thirty. Her husband, older than she, was the one who had first made the acquaintance, but he was abroad on business at the moment. Her children were in the house in London, safe and well cared for.

"My dear Vespasia, you are quite ravishing," Omegus said with a self-deprecating smile. "Of which you cannot fail to be aware, so please do not insult my intelligence by pretending surprise, or worse still, denial." He was a lean man with a wry face, full of humor and an unconscious elegance as much at home in a country lane as a London withdrawing room.

She accepted the compliment with a simple "Thank you." A witty reply would have been inappropriate. Besides, Omegus's candor had robbed her of the ability to think of one.

A dozen people were here, including herself. The most socially prominent were Lord and Lady Salchester, closely followed by Sir John and Lady Warburton. Lady Warburton's sister had married a duke, as she found a dozen ways of reminding people. Actually Vespasia's father had been an earl, but she never spoke of it. It was birth, not achievement, and those who mattered already knew. To remind people was indelicate, as if you had no other worth to yourself, never mind to them.

Also present were Fenton and Blanche Twyford; two eminently eligible young men, Peter Hanning and Bertie Rosythe; Gwendolen Kilmuir, widowed more than a year ago; and Isobel Alvie, whose husband had died nearly three years earlier.

It was not customary to serve refreshments before dinner, but rather simply to converse until the butler should sound the gong. The guests would then go into the dining room in strict order of precedence, the rules for which were set out in the finest detail and must never be broken.

Lady Salchester, a formidable horsewoman, was dressed in a deep wine shade, with a crinoline skirt of daunting proportions. She was speaking of last season's races, in particular the meeting at Royal Ascot.

"Magnificent creature!" she said enthusiastically, her voice booming a little. "Nothing else stood a chance."

Lady Warburton smiled as if in agreement.

Bertie Rosythe — slender, fair, superbly tailored — was trying to mask his boredom, and doing it rather well. If Vespasia had not known him, she might have been duped into imagining he was interested in horseflesh.

Isobel was beside her, darkly striking, less than beautiful but with fine eyes and a ready wit.

"Magnificent creature indeed," she whispered. "And Lady Salchester herself certainly never had a chance."

"What are you talking about?" Vespasia asked, knowing that there must be many layers to the remark.

"Fanny Oakley," Isobel replied, leaning even more closely. "Didn't you see her at Ascot? Whatever were you doing?"

"Watching the horses," Vespasia answered dryly.

"Don't be absurd!" Isobel laughed. "Good heavens! You didn't have money on them, did you? I mean real money?"

Vespasia saw by Isobel's face that she was suddenly concerned in case Vespasia were in gambling debt, not an unheard-of difficulty for a young woman of considerable means and very little to occupy herself, her husband away a good deal of the time, and endless staff to care for her home and her children.

Vespasia wondered for a chill moment if Isobel were really acute enough in her observation to have seen the vague, sad stirrings of emptiness in Vespasia's marriage, and to have at least half understood them. One wished to have friends — without them life would hold only shallow pleasures — but there were areas of the heart into which one did not intrude. Some aches could be borne only in secret. Isobel could not have guessed what had happened in Rome during the passionate revolutions of 1848. No one could. That was a once-in-a-lifetime love, to be buried now and thought of only in dreams. Vespasia would not meet Mario Corena again. This here in Applecross was the world of reality.

"Not at all," she replied lightly. "The race does not need the edge of money to make it fun."

"Are you referring to the horses?" Isobel asked softly.

"Was there another?" Vespasia retorted.

Isobel laughed.

Lord Salchester saw Vespasia and acknowledged her appreciatively. Lady Salchester smiled with warm lips and a glacial eye. "Good evening, Lady Vespasia," she said with penetrating clarity. "How charming to see you. You seem quite recovered from the exertion of the season." It was a less-than-kind reference to a summer cold that had made Vespasia tired and far from herself at the Henley Regatta. "Let us hope next year is not too strenuous for you," she added. She was twenty years older than Vespasia, but a woman of immense stamina who had never been beautiful.

Vespasia was aware of Lord Salchester's eye on her, and even more of Omegus Jones's. It was the latter that tempered her reply. Wit was not always funny, if it cut those already wounded. "I hope so," she answered. "It is tedious for everybody when someone cannot keep up. I shall endeavor not to do that again."

Isobel was surprised. Lady Salchester was astounded.

Vespasia smiled sweetly and excused herself.

Gwendolen Kilmuir was talking earnestly to Bertie Rosythe. Her head was bent a trifle, the light shining on her rich brown hair and the deep plum pink of her gown. She was widowed well over a year now, and had only recently taken the opportunity to cast aside her black. She was a young woman, barely twenty-eight, and had no intention of spending longer in mourning than society demanded. She looked up demurely at Bertie, but she was smiling, and her face had a softness and a warmth to it that was hard to mistake.

Vespasia glanced at Isobel and caught a pensive look in her eye.

Then a moment later she smiled, and it was gone.

Bertie turned and saw them. As always he was gracefully polite. Gwendolen's pleasure was not as easily assumed. Vespasia saw the muscles in her neck and chin tighten and her bosom swell as she breathed deeply before mustering a smile. "Good evening, Lady Vespasia, Mrs. Alvie. How nice it will be to dine together."

"As always," Isobel murmured. "I believe we dined at Lady Cranbourne's also, during the summer? And at the queen's garden party." Her eyes flickered up and down Gwendolen's plum taffeta. "I remember your gown."

Gwendolen blushed. Bertie smiled uncertainly.

Suddenly and with a considerable

jolt, Vespasia realized that Isobel's interest in Bertie was not as casual as she had supposed. The barb in her remark betrayed her. Such cruelty was not in the character she knew.

"You remember her gown?" she said in feigned surprise. "How delightful." She looked with slight disdain at Isobel's russet gold with its sweeping skirts. "So few gowns are remarkable these days, don't you think?"

Isobel caught her breath, a flare of temper in her eyes.

Gwendolen laughed with a release of tension and turned to Bertie again.

Lady Warburton joined them, and the conversation became enmeshed in gossip, cases of "he said" and "she said" and "do you really believe?"

Dinner was announced, and

Omegus Jones offered his arm to Vespasia, which in view of Lady Salchester's presence she found a singular honor, and they went into the long blue-and-gold dining room in solemn and correct procession, each to their appointed place at the glittering table.

The chandeliers above were reflected in the gleam of silver, shattered prisms of light on tiers of crystal goblets in a field of linen napkins folded like lilies. The fire burned warm in the grate. White chrysanthemums from the greenhouse filled the bowls, providing a redolence of earth and autumn leaves, the soft fragrance of woodland.

They began with the lightest consommé. There would be nine courses, but it was not expected that everyone would eat from all of them. Ladies in particular, mindful of the delicate figures and tiny waists demanded by fashion, would choose with care. Where physical survival was relatively easy, one created rules to make social survival more difficult. Not to be accepted was to become an outcast, a person who fitted nowhere.

Conversation turned to more serious topics. Sir John Warburton spoke of the current political situation, giving his views with gravity, his thin hands brown against the white linen of the cloth.

"Do you really think it will come to war?" Peter Hanning asked with a frown.

"With Russia?" Sir John raised his eyebrows. "It is not impossible."

"Nonsense!" Lord Salchester said

briskly, his wineglass in the air. "Nobody's going to go to war against us! Especially over something as absurd as the Crimea! They'll remember Waterloo, and leave us well alone."

"Waterloo was over thirty-five years ago," Omegus Jones pointed out. "The men who fought that have laid their swords by long ago."

"The British army is still the same, sir!" Salchester retorted, his mustache bristling.

"Indeed, I fear it is," Omegus agreed quietly, his lips tight, his eyes sad and far away.

"That was the finest, most invincible army in the world." Salchester's voice grew louder.

"We beat Napoleon," Omegus corrected. "We have fought no one since then. Times change. Good and evil do not, nor pride and compassion, but warfare moves all the time — new weapons, new ideas, new strategies."

"I do not like to disagree with you at your own table, sir," Salchester responded. "Courtesy prevents me from telling you what I think of your view."

Omegus's face lit with a sudden smile, remarkably sweet and quite unaffected. "Let us hope that nothing happens to prove which one of us is correct."

Footmen in livery and parlor maids with white lace-trimmed aprons removed the soup plates and served the fish. The butler poured wine. The lights blazed. The clink of silver on porcelain was the soft background as conversation began again.

Vespasia watched rather than listened. Faces, gestures told her more of emotion than the carefully considered words. She saw how often Gwendolen looked toward Bertie Rosythe, the flush in her face, how easily she laughed when he was amusing, and that it pleased him. He was almost as much aware of her, although he was more careful not to show it quite so openly.

Vespasia was not the only person to notice. She saw Blanche Twyford's satisfaction and recalled hearing her make a remark, which now she understood more clearly. Blanche had spoken of spring weddings, and Gwendolen had blushed. Perhaps this was the weekend when a declaration was expected? It would seem so.

Fenton Twyford seemed less pleased. His dark face looked cautious. A couple of times his glance at Bertie suggested unease, as if an old shadow crossed his thoughts, but Vespasia had no idea what it might be. Was Bertie not quite as perfectly eligible as he seemed? Or was it Gwendolen who somehow fell short? As far as Vespasia knew, she was of good family, wealthy if undistinguished, and without a breath of scandal attached. Her late husband, Roger Kilmuir, was also without blemish and was connected to the aristocracy. If his far elder brother died childless, which seemed likely, then Roger would have inherited the title and all that went with it.

Only, Roger had died in an unfortunate accident, the sort of thing that happened now and again to even the best horsemen. Gwendolen had been quite shattered at the time. It was good to see that she was reaching after some kind of happiness again.

One by one gold-rimmed plates were removed, fresh courses brought, and more wine poured, until nothing was left but mounds of fresh grapes from the hothouse, and silver finger bowls to remove any faint traces of stickiness.

The ladies excused themselves to the withdrawing room and left the gentlemen to pass the port and, for those who so wished, to smoke.

Vespasia followed Isobel and Lady Salchester and was aware of the rustle of taffetas and silks as Gwendolen and Blanche Twyford came behind them. They took their seats in the velvet-curtained withdrawing room, carefully arranging mountainous skirts both to be flattering and not to impede other people's approach, when the gentlemen should rejoin them.

This was the part of any evening that Vespasia liked the least. Conversation almost always became domestic, and since Rome she found it hard to concentrate on such things. She loved her children, deeply and instinctively, and her marriage was agreeable enough. Her husband was kind and intelligent — an honorable man. Many women would have been envious of so much. She wanted for nothing socially or materially. It was only in the longing of the heart, the hunger to care to the power and depth of her being, that she was not answered.

She looked at the other women in

the room and wondered what lay behind the gracious masks of their faces. Lady Salchester had energy and intelligence, but she was plain, plainer than her own parlor maid, and probably the housemaid and the kitchen maid, as well. It was widely suspected that Lord Salchester's attention wandered, in a practical as well as imaginary way.

"I know what you are thinking," Isobel said beside her, leaning a little closer so she could speak in a whisper.

Vespasia was startled. "Do you?"

"Of course!" Isobel smiled. "I was thinking so, too. And it is quite unfair. If she were to do the same, with that nice-looking footman, society would be scandalized, and she would be ruined. She would never go anywhere again!"

"Dozens of married women become bored with their husbands, and after they have produced the appropriate number of children, they have affairs," Vespasia pointed out sadly. "I don't think I admire it, but I am quite aware that it occurs. I could name you half a dozen."

"So could I," Isobel agreed flippantly. "We'll have to do it, and see if we know the same ones."

Blanche Twyford was talking to Gwendolen, nodding every now and then, and Gwendolen was smiling. It was easy to guess the subject of their excitement.

Vespasia looked sideways at Isobel and saw the shadow in her eyes again. If Bertie proposed marriage to Gwendolen this weekend, which seemed to be generally expected, would Isobel really lose more than a possible admirer? Did she care for him, perhaps even have hopes herself? She had loved her husband; Vespasia knew that. But he had been gone for three years now, and Isobel was a young woman, no more than Vespasia's own age. It was possible to fall in love again. In fact, at thirty it would be harsh and lonely not to.

Should she say something? Was this a time when real friendship dared embarrassment and rejection? Or was silence, the pretense of not knowing, preferable, thereby allowing the deeper wounds to remain private?

The decision was taken from her by the arrival of Lady Warburton, whereupon the conversation moved to fashion, Prince Albert's latest ideas for improving the mind, and, of course, the queen's enthusiasm for everything her husband said.

They were rejoined by the gentlemen, and the atmosphere changed again. Everyone became more self-conscious, backs a little straighter, laughter more delicate, movement more graceful. The servants had retreated to leave them alone. The final cleaning up would be done when the guests retired to bed.

They were all facing Gwendolen and Bertie when Isobel made the remark. Gwendolen was sitting with her skirts swept around her like a tide, her head up, her slender throat pale in the candlelight. She looked beautiful and triumphant. Bertie stood close to her, just a little possessively.

"Charming," Lady Warburton said very quietly, as if the announcement had already been made.

Vespasia looked at Isobel and saw the strain in her face. She felt a moment's deep sorrow for her. Whatever the prize, defeat is a bitter taste.

Peter Hanning was saying something trivial, and everyone laughed. There was a goblet of water on the side table. Gwendolen asked for it.

Bertie reached across swiftly and picked it up, then set it on the tray, which had been left there. He passed it to her, balanced in one hand, bowing as he did so. "Madame," he said humbly. "Your servant forever."

Gwendolen put out her hand.

"For heaven's sake, you look like a footman!" Isobel's voice was clear and brittle. "Surely you aspire to be more than that? She's hardly going to give her favors to a servant! At least, not permanently!"

The moment froze. It was a dreadful statement, and Vespasia winced.

"She will require a gentleman," Isobel went on. "After all, Kilmuir could look forward to a title." She turned to Gwendolen. "Couldn't he?"

Gwendolen was white. "I love the man," she said huskily. "The status means nothing to me."

Isobel raised her eyebrows very high. "You would give yourself to him if he were really a footman?" she asked incredulously. "My dear, I believe you!"

Gwendolen stared at her, but her gaze was inward, as if she saw a horror beyond description, almost beyond endurance. Then slowly she rose to her feet, her eyes hollow. She seemed a trifle unsteady.

"Gwendolen!" Bertie said quickly, but she walked past him as if suddenly he were invisible to her. She stumbled to the door, needing a moment or two to grasp the handle and turn it, then went out into the hall.

Lady Warburton turned on Isobel. "Really, Mrs. Alvie, I know you imagine that you are amusing, at least at times, but that remark merely exposed your envy, and it is most unbecoming." She swiveled to face Omegus Jones. "If you will excuse me, I shall make sure that poor Gwendolen is all right." And with a crackle of skirts she swept out.

There was an uncomfortable silence. Vespasia decided to take control before the situation degenerated. She turned to Isobel. "I don't think this can be salvaged with any grace. We would do better to retreat and leave well enough alone. Come. It is late anyway."

Isobel hesitated only a moment, glancing at the ring of startled and embarrassed faces, and realized she could only agree.

Outside in the hall Vespasia took her arm, forcing her to stop before she reached the bottom of the stairs. "What on earth has got hold of you?" she demanded. "You will have to apologize to Gwendolen tomorrow, and to everyone else. Being in love with Bertie does not excuse what you did, and you would be a great deal better off if you had not made yourself so obvious!"

Isobel glared at her, her face ashen but for the high spots of color in her cheeks, but she was too close to tears to answer. She was now perfectly aware of how foolish she had been, and that she had made not Gwendolen but herself look vulnerable. She shook her arm free and stormed up the stairs without looking backwards.

Vespasia did not sleep well. Certainly Isobel had behaved most unfortunately, but marriage, with love or without it, was a very serious business. For a woman it was the only honorable occupation, and battles for an eligible man of the charm and the financial means of someone like

Bertie Rosythe were fought to the last ditch. She hurt for the pain Isobel must feel, a pain she had just made a great deal worse for herself. Vespasia could only imagine it. Her own marriage had been easily arranged. Her father was an earl, and she herself was startlingly beautiful. She could have been a duchess had she wished. She preferred a man of intelligence and an ambition to do something useful, and who loved her for herself and gave her a great deal of freedom. It was a good bargain. The kind of love for which she hungered was well lost and offered to very few — and belonged in dreams and hot Roman summers of manning the barricades against overwhelming odds. One loves utterly, and then yields to honor and duty and returns home to live with other realities, leaving the height and the ache of passion behind.

She rose in the morning and, with her maid's assistance of course, dressed warmly in a blue-gray woolen gown against the December frost and a very sharp wind whining in the eaves and seeking to find every crack in the windows. She went downstairs to face the other guests and whatever difficulties the night had not resolved.

She was met in the hall by Omegus Jones. He was wearing an outdoor jacket and there was mud on his boots. His dark hair was untidy, and his face was so pale he looked waxen.

"Vespasia . . ."

"Whatever is it?" She went to him immediately. "You look ill! Can I help?" She touched his hand lightly.

It was freezing — and wet. Suddenly she was frightened. Omegus, more than anyone else she knew, always seemed in control of himself, and of events. "What is it?" she said again, more urgently.

He did not prevaricate. He closed his icy hand over hers with great gentleness. "I am afraid we have just found Gwendolen's body in the lake." He gestured vaguely behind him to the sheet of ornamental water beyond the sloping lawn with its cedars and herbaceous border. "We have brought her out, but there is nothing to be done for her. She seems to have been dead since sometime last night."

Vespasia was stunned. It was impossible. "How can she have fallen in?" she said, denying the thought desperately. "It is shallow at the edges. There are flowers growing there, reeds! You would simply get stuck in the mud! And anyway, why on earth would she go walking down by the water on a December night? Why would anyone?"

He looked haggard, and he was unmoved by her arguments, except to pity.

Vespasia was touched by a deep fear.

"I'm sorry, my dear," he answered, his eyes hollow. "She went in from the bridge, where it is quite deep. The only conclusion possible seems to be that she jumped, of her own accord. The balustrade is quite high enough to prevent an accidental falling, even in the dark. I had them made that way myself."

"Omegus! I'm so sorry!" Her first thought was for him, and the distress it would cause him, the dark shadow over the beauty of Applecross. It was a loveliness more than simply that of a great house where art and nature had combined to create a perfect landscape of flowers, trees, water, and views to the hills and fields beyond. It was a place of peace where generations of love of the land had sunk into its fabric and left a residue of warmth, even in the starkness of late autumn.

Approached from the southwest along an avenue of towering elms, the classic Georgian facade looked toward the afternoon sun over the downs. The gravel forecourt was fronted by a balustrade with a long, shallow flight of stone steps that led down to the vast lawn, beyond which lay the ornamental water.

"I'm afraid it will become most unpleasant," he said unhappily. "People will be frightened because sudden death of the young is a terrible reminder of the fragility of all life. She had seemed on the brink of new joy after her bereavement, and it has been snatched away from her. Only the boldest of us, and the least imaginative, do not sometimes in the small hours of the morning also fear the same for ourselves. And they will not understand why it has happened. They will look for someone to blame, because anger is easier to live with than fear."

"I don't understand!" she said with a gulp. "Why on earth would she do such a thing? Isobel was cruel, but if anyone should be mortified, it is she! She betrayed her own vulnerability in front of those who will have no understanding and little mercy."

"We know that, my dear Vespasia, but they do not," he said softly, still touching her so lightly she felt only the coldness of his fingers. "They will see only a woman with every cause to expect an offer of marriage, but who was publicly insulted by suggestions that she is a seeker after position rather than a woman in love." His face twisted with irony. "Which is an absurd piece of hypocrisy, I am aware. We have created a society in which it is necessary for a woman to marry well if she is to succeed, because we have contrived for it to be impossible for her to achieve any safety or success alone, even should she wish to. But frequently we criticize most vehemently that which is largely our own doing."

"Are you . . . are you saying that Isobel's remark drove her to commit suicide?" Vespasia's voice cracked as if her mouth and throat were parched.

"It seems so," he admitted. "Unless there was an exchange between Bertie and Gwendolen after she left the withdrawing room, and a quarrel she did not feel she could repair."

Vespasia could think of nothing to say. It was hideous.

"You offered to help me," Omegus reminded her. "I may ask that you do."

"How?"

"I have very little idea," he confessed. "Perhaps that is why I need you."

Vespasia swallowed hard. "I shall tell Isobel," she said, wondering how on earth she could make such a thing bearable. The day yawned ahead like an abyss, full of grief and confusion.

"Thank you," he accepted. "I shall have the servants ask everyone to be at breakfast, and tell them then."

She nodded, then turned and went back upstairs and along to Isobel's room. She knocked on the door and waited until she heard Isobel's voice tell her to go in.

Isobel was lying in the bed, her dark hair spread across the pillow, her eyes shadowed around as if she, too, had slept badly. She sat up slowly, staring at Vespasia in surprise.

There was no mercy in hesitation. Vespasia sat on the bed facing Isobel. "I have just met Omegus in the hall,"

she began. "They have found Gwendolen's body in the lake. The only
conclusion possible from the circumstances is that sometime after our unfortunate conversation in the
withdrawing room she must have
gone out alone and, in some derange-
ment of mind, jumped off the bridge.
I'm afraid it is very bad."

Isobel sat up, pulling the sheet
around herself, even though the room
was not cold. "Is she . . . ?"

"Of course. It is December! If she
had not drowned, she would have
frozen."

"But surely she must have fallen!"
Isobel protested, pushing her hair off
her face. "Why on earth would she
jump? That's ridiculous!" She shook
her head. "It can't be true!"

"If you remember, the balustrade

47

along the bridge is too high to fall over by accident," Vespasia reminded her. "Anyway, why on earth would she be out there leaning over the bridge at eleven o'clock on a December night? And alone!"

The little color in Isobel's face had drained away, leaving her pasty-white. She started to shiver. Her hands were clenched in the sheets.

"Are you implying that my idiotic remark made her do that? Why? All I did was insult her! She wouldn't be the first woman to be called greedy, or desperate. That's absurd!" Her voice was sharp, a little high-pitched.

"Isobel, there is no point in pretending that it did not happen," Vespasia said steadily, trying to sound reasonable, although she did not feel it. "You are going to have to go down at some time and face everyone, whatever they believe. And the longer you delay it, the more you will appear to be accepting the blame."

"I'm not to blame!" Isobel said indignantly. "I was rash in what I said, and I would have apologized to her today. But if she went and jumped off the bridge, that has nothing to do with me, and I won't have anyone say that it has!" She flung the sheets aside and climbed out of the bed, stumbling a little as she stood up. She kept her back to Vespasia, as though blaming her for having brought the news. But Vespasia noticed that when Isobel picked up her peignoir, her fingers were stiff, and when it slipped out of her grasp, it took her three attempts to retrieve it.

Breakfast was ghastly. When Vespasia and Isobel arrived, everyone else was already gathered around the table. Food was laid out on the sideboard in silver chafing dishes: finnan haddock, kedgeree, eggs, sausage, deviled kidneys, and bacon. There was also plenty of fresh crisp toast, butter, marmalade, and tea. People had served themselves, as a matter of good manners, before Omegus Jones had divulged what had occurred, but nobody felt like eating.

Isobel's entrance had been greeted in silence, nor did anyone meet her eyes.

Vespasia looked at Omegus and saw the warning and the apology unspoken in his expression.

Isobel hesitated. No one was wearing black, because no one had foreseen the occasion, and of course Isobel was the only one who had known of the death before dressing. She wore a sober dark green.

Lady Warburton was the first to acknowledge her presence, but it was with a chilly stare, her rather ordinary face pinched with distaste. She regarded Isobel's clothes first, long before her face. "I see you were aware of the tragedy before you dressed," she said coolly. "In fact, perhaps last night?"

"My dear Evelyn, do not let your grief . . . ," Sir John began, then trailed away as his wife turned to glare at him.

"It is perfectly obvious she was

aware of poor Gwendolen's death!" she said in a low, grating voice. "Why else would she wear mourning to breakfast?"

"Hypocrite," Blanche Twyford murmured half under her breath. No one doubted that she was referring to Isobel, not Lady Warburton.

Isobel pretended not to have heard. She took a slice of toast, and then found herself unable to swallow it. She played with it to keep her hands occupied, and perhaps to prevent anyone else from noticing that they trembled.

Bertie looked haggard and utterly confused.

Vespasia wondered if he had gone after Gwendolen last night. Surely he must have. Or was it conceivable he had not? If he had followed her and told her of his feelings, asked her to marry him as everyone was expecting, nothing Isobel Alvie, or anyone else, could have said would have destroyed her happiness. Was that what he was thinking, that he avoided her eyes now? And what about Lady Warburton? Had she followed Gwendolen, or merely said she would to escape the situation?

"This is perfectly dreadful!" Lady Salchester burst out. "We really cannot sit here not knowing what has happened, and having no idea what to say to each other!"

"We know what has happened," Blanche Twyford said angrily. "Mrs. Alvie spoke inexcusably last night, and poor Mrs. Kilmuir was so distraught that she took her own life. It's as plain as the nose on your face."

Lady Salchester froze. "I beg your pardon?" she said, ice dripping from her voice.

"For heaven's sake!" Blanche flushed. "I did not mean it personally. It is an expression of — of clarity. We all know perfectly well what happened!"

"I don't." Lord Salchester came surprisingly to his wife's aid. "To me it is as much of a muddle as the nose on your face!"

Vespasia wanted to laugh hysterically. She suppressed the desire with difficulty, holding her napkin to her lips and pretending to sneeze.

Blanche Twyford glared at Lord Salchester.

Salchester opened his blue eyes very wide. "Why on earth should a perfectly healthy young woman on the brink of matrimony throw herself into the lake? Merely because her rival insults her? I don't understand." He looked baffled. He shook his head. "Women," he said unhappily. "If she had been a chap, she'd simply have insulted her back, and they'd have gone to bed friends."

"Oh, do be quiet, Ernest!" Lady Salchester snapped at him. "You are talking complete nonsense!"

"Am I?" he said mildly. "Wasn't she going to be married? That's what everyone said!"

Bertie stood up, white-faced, and left the room.

"Good God! He's not going to the lake, is he?" Salchester asked, his napkin sliding to the floor.

Isobel left the table, as well, only she went out the other door, toward the garden, even though it was raining and not much above freezing outside.

"Guilt!" Lady Warburton said viciously.

"I think that's a little harsh," Sir John expostulated. "She was —"

"Both of them!" his wife cut across, effectively cutting off whatever he had been going to say. He lapsed into silence.

Omegus rose to his feet. "Lady Vespasia, I wonder if I might talk with you in the library?"

"Of course." She was grateful for the chance to escape the ghastly meal table. She scraped her chair back before the footman could pull it out for her.

"You're not going to just leave it!" Lady Warburton accused him. "This cannot be run away from. I won't allow it!"

Omegus looked at her coldly. "I am going to think before I act, Lady Warburton. An error now, even if made with the purest of motives, could cause grief which could not later be undone. Excuse me." And leaving her angry, and now confounded, he left the room with Vespasia at his heels.

In the silence of the book-lined library with its exquisite bronzes he closed the door and turned to face her. "Evelyn Warburton is right," he said grimly. There was intense sadness in his eyes, and the lines around his mouth were drawn down.

"It was foolish," she agreed. "And unkind. Both are faults, but not in any way crimes, or most of society would be in prison. It is dreadful that Gwendolen should have taken her life, but surely it is because she believed that Bertie would not marry her after all? It cannot be simply that Isobel behaved so badly."

He regarded her with patience. "It is not necessarily what is but what is perceived that society will judge," he answered. "Whether it is fair or not will enter into it very little. If we allow it to pass without addressing it, each time it is retold it will grow worse. What Isobel actually said will be lost in the exaggerations until no one remembers the truth. Tales alter every time they are retold, and, my dear, you must know that." There was a faint reproof in his voice.

Of course she knew it, and felt the color burn in her face for her evasion.

"What can we do?" she said help-lessly. "What do you suppose the truth is? And how will we ever know? Gwendolen can't tell us, and if Bertie quarreled with her, do you imagine he will tell us, in view of what has happened? Did Lady Warburton go after her? Do you know?"

"Apparently not. Do you know anything of medieval trials when someone was accused of a crime?" he asked.

She was astounded. Surely he could not have said what she thought she had heard. "I beg your pardon?"

Somewhere in the garden a dog was barking, and a servant's rapid foot-steps crossed the hall. The ghost of a smile curved his lips. "I am not refer-ring to trial by combat, or by ordeal. I was thinking of a process of discovering the truth so far as we are able. If Isobel is indeed guilty of anything, or if Bertie is, then all of us agreeing upon a form of expiation would absolve them of guilt, after which we would make a solemn covenant that the matter would be considered closed."

A wild hope flared up inside her. "But would we?" she said, struggling to believe it. "Would we agree to it? And could we find the truth? What if the guilty person would not accept the expiation?" She lifted her shoulders very slightly. "And what could it be? What if they simply walk away? We have no power to enforce anything. Why should they trust us to keep silent afterwards, let alone to forgive?"

He walked over to the heavy velvet

curtains and the window overlooking the parkland with its rolling grass and great trees, now winter bare. Rain spattered against the glass.

"I have thought about it," he said, as much to himself as to her. "The idea always appealed to me, the belief in expiation and forgiveness, a new start. Surely that is the only hope for any of us. We need both to forgive and to be forgiven."

Looking at him standing with the harsh light on his face, she saw more pain inside him than she had in the years she had known him, and also a far greater understanding of peace. In that instant she wished above all to fulfill this faith in her, to make him pleased that it was she to whom he had turned.

"But why should they agree?" she

said anxiously. "We have no power other than persuasion."

He smiled and turned to face her. "Oh, but we have! The power of society is almost infinite, my dear. To be excluded is a kind of death. And if one is spoken of with sufficient venom, invitations cease, doors are closed, and one becomes invisible. People pass one by without a glance. One finds that in all ways that matter, one no longer exists. A young woman becomes unmarriageable. A young man has no career, no position; all clubs are closed to him."

It was true. Vespasia had seen it. It was the cruelest fate because the people to whom it could happen were unfitted for any other life. They did not know how to earn a living in the work done by ordinary men and women. Those occupations also were closed to them. No woman born a lady could suddenly become a maid or a laundress. Even had she the skills, the temperament, and the stamina, she was not acceptable either to an employer of the class she used to be, or to the other employees to whose class she did not belong, nor ever could.

And she was not fitted or trained for any of the other occupations in which a woman could earn her way.

Suddenly Vespasia realized just what might be ahead for Isobel, and she felt cold and sick. "How will that help us?" she said huskily.

He looked at her with great earnestness. "If I explain to everyone what I have in mind, and they agree, then they will all be bound by it," he answered. "The punishment for breaking their word would be exactly that same ostracism which will be applied to whoever is found at fault in Gwendolen's death. Anyone who refuses to abide by that brands himself as outside the group of the rest of us. No one will wish to do that." He shook his head a tiny fraction, lips tight. "Don't tell me it is coercion. I know. Few people accept the judgment of their peers without it. It will offer a way for us to prevent the pain, and perhaps injustice, that may result otherwise." His voice became softer. "And as important, it will at least give Isobel, or Bertie if it is he to blame, a chance to expiate the act of cruelty they may have performed."

"How?" she asked.

"Gwendolen left a letter behind,"

he explained. "It is sealed, and will remain so. It is addressed to her mother, Mrs. Naylor, who lives near Inverness, in the far north of Scotland. We could post it, but that would be a harsh way for a mother to find out that her child has destroyed the life she labored to give."

Vespasia was appalled. "You mean they would have to go to this unhappy woman and give her the letter? That's . . ." She was lost for words. Isobel would never do it! Neither would Bertie Rosythe. They would neither of them have the heart, or the stomach, for it. Not to mention making the journey to the north of Scotland in December.

Omegus raised his eyebrows. "Do you expect to be forgiven without pain, without a pilgrimage that costs the mind, the body, and the heart?"

"I don't think it will work."

"Will you at least help me try?"

She looked at him standing, lean, oddly graceful, the lines deeper in his face in the morning light, and she could not refuse. "Of course."

"Thank you," he said solemnly.

"What?" Lord Salchester said with stinging disbelief when they were gathered together at the luncheon table. The first course was finished when Omegus requested their attention and began to explain to them his plan.

"Preposterous!" Lady Warburton agreed. "We all know perfectly well what happened. For heaven's sake, we saw it!"

"Heard it," Sir John corrected.

She glared at him.

"Actually," he went on. "It's not a bad idea at all."

Lady Warburton swung around in her chair and fixed him with a glacial eye. "It is ridiculous. And if we find Mrs. Alvie guilty, as we will do, what difference will that make?"

"That is not the end of the issue," Omegus exclaimed. Vespasia saw him struggling to keep the dislike from his face. "In medieval times not all crimes were punished by execution or imprisonment," he went on. "Sometimes the offender was permitted to make a pilgrimage of expiation. If he returned, which in those dangerous times very often he did not, then the sin was considered to have been washed out. All men were bound to pardon it and take the person back among them as if it had not occurred. It was never spoken of again, and he was trusted and loved as before."

"A pilgrimage?" Peter Hanning said with disbelief, derision close to laughter in his voice. "To where, for heaven's sake? Walsingham? Canterbury? Jerusalem, perhaps? Anyway, travel is a relative pleasure these days, if one can afford it. I'm not a religious man. I don't care a fig if Mrs. Alvie, or anyone else, makes a journey to some holy place."

"You have missed the point, Peter," Omegus told him. "I shall choose the journey, and it will not be a pleasure. Nor will it be particularly expensive. But it will be extremely difficult, particularly so for anyone who bears guilt at all for the death of Gwendolen Kilmuir. And if we profess any claim to justice whatsoever, we will not decide in advance who that is."

"I agree," Sir John said immediately.

"So do I," Vespasia added. "I agree to both justice and forgiveness."

"And if I don't?" Lady Warburton asked sharply, looking across at Vespasia, her brow creased with dislike, her mouth pinched.

Vespasia smiled. "Then one would be compelled to wonder why not," she replied.

"I agree," Blanche Twyford said. "Then it need never be spoken of beyond these walls. It will stop gossip among others who were not here, and any slander they may make against any of us, letting their imaginations build all manner of speculation. If we are all bound by what we agree, and the punishment is carried out here, the matter is ours. Surely you agree, don't you?"

"I suppose, if you put it that way," Lady Warburton said reluctantly.

Lord Salchester agreed also.

Omegus looked at Bertie, the question in his face.

"Who is to be the judge of this?" Bertie asked dubiously. Today his elegance seemed haggard, his exquisite suit and cravat an irrelevance.

"Omegus," Vespasia said before anyone else could speak. "He is not involved and we may trust him to be fair."

"May we?" Bertie said. "Applecross is his house. He is most certainly involved."

"He is not involved in Gwendolen's death." Vespasia kept her temper with increasing difficulty. "Do you have someone in mind you prefer?"

"I think the whole idea is absurd," he replied. "And totally impractical."

"I disagree." Lord Salchester spoke with sudden decisiveness, his voice sharp. "I think it is an excellent idea. I am quite happy to be bound by it. So is my wife." He did not consult her. "It will be for the good of all our reputations, and will allow the matter to be dealt with immediately, and justice be served." He looked a little balefully around the table at the others. "Who is against it? Apart from those either guilty or too shortsighted to see the ultimate good."

Omegus smiled bleakly, but he did

not point out the loaded nature of the challenge. One by one they all agreed, except Isobel.

Vespasia looked at her very steadily. "Any alternative would be much worse, I believe," she said softly. "Do we all give our word, on pain of being ostracized ourselves should we break it, that we will keep silence, absolutely, on the subject after the judgment is given and should the price be paid? Then the offender, if there is one, begins anew from the day of their return, and we forget the offense as if it had not happened?"

One by one, reluctantly at first, they each gave their pledge.

"Thank you," Omegus said gravely. "Then after luncheon we shall begin."

They collected in the withdrawing room, the curtains open on the formal garden sweeping down toward the wind-ruffled water of the lake, and the trees beyond. It was the place where they could all be seated in something close to a circle, and the servants were dismissed until they should be called for. No one was to interrupt.

Omegus called them to order, then asked each of them in turn to tell what they knew of Gwendolen Kilmuir's actions, her feelings, and what she may have said to them of her hopes from the time she had arrived three days before.

They began tentatively, unsure

how far to trust, but gradually emotions were stirred by memory.

"She was full of hope," Blanche said a little tearfully. "She believed that her time of loss was coming to an end." She shot a look of intense dislike at Isobel. "Kilmuir's death was a terrible blow to her."

"So much so that she intended to marry less than a year and a half later," Peter Hanning observed, leaning back in his chair, his cravat a little crooked, a slight curl to his lip.

"They had had some difficult times," Blanche explained crossly. "He was not an easy man."

"It was she who was not an easy woman," Fenton Twyford interrupted. "She took some time to accept her responsibilities. Kilmuir was very patient with her, but the time came when he bore it less graciously."

"A great deal less graciously," Blanche agreed. "But he was mending his ways. She was looking forward to a far greater warmth between them when he was killed."

"Killed?" Sir John said abruptly.

"In an accident," Blanche told him. "A horse bolted, I believe, and he was thrown out of the trap and dragged. Quite dreadful. When she heard of it, poor Gwendolen was devastated. That was why it was so wonderful that she had a second chance at happiness." She looked at Bertie with intense meaning.

He blushed miserably.

The tale progressed, each person adding colorful details until a picture emerged of the courtship of Bertie and Gwendolen, reaching the point when everyone expected an announcement. More than one person had noticed that Isobel was not pleased, even though she attempted to hide the fact. Now all the thoughts came to the surface, and she was clearly humiliated, but she did not dare escape. It would have been an admission, and she was determined not to make one.

But the tide swept relentlessly on. Even Vespasia was carried along by it until she was placed in a position where she must speak either for Isobel or against her. She had been forced to see more clearly now than at the time how deep the feelings had been on both sides. Under the veneer of wit and a kind of friendship, there had been a struggle for victory, which would have lifted either one woman or the other back onto the crest of a wave in society, assured of comfort and acceptance. The other would be left among the number of women alone, always a little apart, a little lost, hoping for the next invitation, but never certain that it would come, dreading the next bill in case it would not be met.

Without realizing why, Vespasia spoke for Isobel. Gwendolen was beyond her help, and many others were eager to take her part.

"We use what arts we have," she said, looking more at Omegus than the others. "Gwendolen was pretty and charming. She flattered people by allowing them to help her, and she was grateful. Isobel was far too proud for that, and too honest. She used wit, and sometimes it was cruel. I think when Gwendolen was the victim, she affected to be more wounded than she was. She craved sympathy, and she won it. Isobel was foolish enough not to see that."

"If Gwendolen was not really hurt, why did she kill herself?" Blanche demanded angrily, challenge in her eyes and the set of her thin shoulders. "That seems to be taking the cry for sympathy rather too far to be of any use!" Her voice was heavily sarcastic, her smile a sneer.

Vespasia looked at Bertie. "When Gwendolen left last night, after Isobel's remark, did you go after her to see if she was all right?" she asked him. "Did you assure her that you did not for an instant believe she was in love with your money and position rather than with you?"

Bertie colored painfully and his face tightened.

Everyone waited.

"Did you?" Omegus said in a very clear voice.

Bertie looked up. "No. I admit it. Isobel spoke with such . . . certainty, I did wonder. I, God forgive me, I doubted her." He fidgeted. "I started to think of things she had said, things other people had said — warnings." He tried to laugh and failed. "Of course, I realize now that they were merely malicious, born of jealousy. But last night I hesitated. If I hadn't, poor Gwendolen would be alive, and I should not be alone, mourning her loss." The look he gave Isobel was venomous in its intensity and its blame.

Vespasia was stunned. It was the

last response she had intended to provoke. Far from helping Isobel, she had sealed her fate.

Omegus also looked wretched, but he was bound by his own rules.

The verdict was a matter of form. By overwhelming majority they found Isobel guilty of unbridled cruelty and deliberate intent to ruin Gwendolen, falsely, in the eyes of the man she loved. There was sympathy for Bertie, but it was not unmixed with a certain contempt.

"And what is this pilgrimage that Mrs. Alvie is to make?" Fenton Twyford asked angrily. "I must say I agree with Peter. I really don't care where she goes, as long as it is not across my path. I can't stand a woman with a vicious tongue. It's inexcusable."

"Very little is inexcusable,"

Omegus said with sudden cutting authority, his face at once bleak and touched with a terrible compassion. "You have given your word before everyone here that if she completes the journey, you will wipe the matter from your memory as if it did not happen. Otherwise, you will have broken your word — and that also cannot be excused. If a man's oath does not bind him, then he cannot be a part of any civilized society."

Twyford went white. He glanced around the table. No one smiled at him. Lord Salchester nodded in agreement. "Quite so," he said. "Quite so."

"Are we agreed?" Omegus inquired softly.

"We are," came the answer from everyone except Isobel.

Omegus turned to her and waited.

"What journey?" she said huskily.

Omegus explained. "Gwendolen left a letter addressed to her mother, Mrs. Naylor. I have not opened it, nor will you. It's obviously private. You will take it to Mrs. Naylor and explain to her that Gwendolen has taken her own life, and your part in it. If Mrs. Naylor wishes to come to London, or to Applecross, you will accompany her, unless she will not permit you to. But you will do all in your power to succeed. She lives near Inverness, in the Highlands of Scotland. Her address is on the envelope."

The silence in the room was broken by the sound of a sudden shower lashing the windows.

"I won't!" Isobel said in a rush of outrage. "The north of Scotland! At this time of year? And to . . . to face . . . absolutely not." She stood up, her body shaking, her face burning with hectic color. "I will not do it." For a moment she stared at them, and then left the room, grasping the door until it slammed against the farther wall, then swinging it shut after her.

Vespasia half rose also, then realized the futility of it and sat down again.

"I thought she wouldn't," Lady Warburton said with a smile of satisfaction.

Vespasia thought for an instant of a crocodile who fears it is robbed of its prey, and then feels its teeth sink into flesh after all. "You must be pleased," she said aloud. "I imagine you would have found it nigh on impossible to know something unkind about someone and be unable to repeat it to others."

Lady Warburton looked at her coldly, her face suddenly bloodless, eyes glittering. "I would be more careful in my choice of friends, if I were you, Lady Vespasia. Your father's title will not protect you forever. There is a degree of foolishness beyond which even you will have to pay."

"You are suggesting I desert my friends the moment it becomes inconvenient to me?" Vespasia inquired, although there was barely an inflection in her tone, only heavy disgust. "Why does it not astound me that you should say so?" She also rose to her feet. "Excuse me," she said to no one in particular, and left the room.

Outside in the hall she was completely alone. There was no servant in sight, no footman waiting to be called. They had taken Omegus's request for privacy as an absolute order. There was something strangely judicial about it, as if everything, even domestic detail, might be different from now on.

She crossed the wooden parquet and climbed slowly up the great staircase. A few words had changed everything. But they were not merely words: They sprang from thoughts and passions, deep tides that had been there all the time; it was only the knowledge of them that was new.

Vespasia found it difficult to concentrate on dressing for dinner. Her maid suggested one gown after another, but nothing seemed appropriate, nor for once did she really care. The silks, laces, embroidery, the whole palette of subtle and gorgeous colors seemed an empty pleasure. Gwendolen was dead, from whatever despair real or imagined that had gripped her, and Isobel was on the brink of suffering more than she yet understood.

She thought everyone else would be dressing soberly, in grief for Gwendolen, and in parade of their sense of social triumph, somber but victorious. She decided to wear purple. It suited her porcelain skin and the shimmering glory of her hair. It would be beautiful, appropriate for half mourning, and outrageous for a woman of her youth. Altogether it would serve every purpose.

She swept down the stairs again, as she had only an evening ago, to gasps of surprise, and either admiration or envy, depending upon whether it was Lord Salchester or Lady Warburton. The merest glance told her that Isobel was not yet there. Would she have the courage to come?

Omegus was at her elbow, his face carefully smoothed of expression, but she could not mistake the anxiety in his eyes.

"She is not going to run away, is she?" he said so quietly that Blanche Twyford, only a yard or two from them, could not have heard.

Vespasia had exactly the same fear. "I don't know," she admitted. "I think she is very angry. There is a certain injustice in putting the blame entirely upon her. If Bertie was so easily put off, then he did not love Gwendolen with much depth or honor."

"Of course not, my dear," Omegus murmured. "Surely that is the disillusion which really hurt Gwendolen more than she could bear."

Suddenly it made agonizing sense. It was not any suggestion Isobel made. It was the exposing of the shallowness beneath the dreams, the breaking of the thin veneer of hope with which Gwendolen had deceived herself. She had not lost the prize; she had seen that it did not exist, not as she needed it to be.

"Was that really a cruelty?" she said aloud, meeting his eyes for the first time in their whispered conversation.

Omegus did not hesitate. "Yes," he answered. "There are some things to which we need to wake up slowly, and the weaknesses of someone we love are among them."

"But surely she needed to see what a frail creature he is before she married him!" she protested.

He smiled. "Oh, please, think a little longer, a little more deeply, my dear."

She was surprisingly wounded, not bluntly as by a knife, but deeply and almost without realizing it for the first few seconds, as a razor cuts. She had not been aware until this moment how much she cared what Omegus thought of her.

Perhaps he saw the change in her face. His expression softened.

She found herself pulling away, her pride offended that he should see his power to wound her.

He saw that, too, and he ignored it. "She would have accepted him," he said, still quietly. "She had no better offer, and by the time she had realized his flaws, he might have begun to overcome them, and habit, tenderness, other promises made and kept might have blunted the edge of disappointment, and given other compensations that would have been enough." He put his hand on her arm, so lightly she saw it rather than felt it. "Love is not perfection," he said. "It is tolerance, dreams past, and the future shared. A great deal of it, my dear, is friendship, if it is to last. There is nothing more precious than true friendship. It is the rock upon which all other loves must stand, if they are to endure. She should have made her own decision, not have it made for her by someone else's desperate realization of defeat."

She did not answer. His words filled her mind and left no room for any of her own.

Ten minutes later when Isobel still had not appeared, Vespasia decided to go and fetch her. She went back up the stairs and along the west corridor to Isobel's room. She knocked and, when there was no answer, turned the handle and went in.

Isobel was standing before the long glass, looking critically at herself. She was not beautiful, but she had a great grace, and in her bronze-and-black gown she looked magnificent, more striking, more dramatic than Gwendolen ever had. Vespasia saw for the first time that that was precisely the trouble. Bertie Rosythe did not want a dramatic wife. He might like to play with fire, but he did not wish to live with it. Isobel could never have won.

"If you do not come now, you are going to be late," Vespasia said calmly.

Isobel swung around, startled. She had obviously been expecting the return of her maid.

"I haven't decided if I am coming yet," she replied. "I didn't hear you knock!"

"I daresay you were too deep in your own thoughts." Vespasia brushed it aside. "You must come," she insisted. "If you don't, you will be seen as having run away, and that would be an admission of guilt."

"They think I am guilty anyway," Isobel said bitterly. "Don't pretend you cannot see that! Even you with so . . ."

Vespasia had been at fault. "I did not intend my remarks to give them that opening," she answered. "I am truly sorry for that. It was far clumsier than I meant it to be."

Isobel kept her head turned away. "I daresay they would have come to the same place anyway, just taken a little longer. But it would have been easier for me had the final blow not come from a friend."

"Then you may consider yourself revenged," Vespasia said. "I am subtly chastened, and guilty of my own sin. Are you now coming down to dinner? The longer you leave it, the more difficult it will be. That is the truth, whoever is to blame for anything."

Isobel turned around very slowly. "Why are you wearing purple, for heaven's sake? Is anyone else in mourning?"

Vespasia smiled bleakly. "Of course not. No one foresaw the necessity of bringing it. I am wearing purple because it suits me."

"Everything suits you!" Isobel retorted.

"No, it doesn't. Everything I wear suits me, because I have enough sense not to wear what doesn't. Now put on your armor, and come to dinner."

"Armor!"

"Courage, dignity, hope — and

enough sense not to speak unless you are spoken to, and not to try to be funny."

"Funny! I couldn't laugh if Lord Salchester performed handstands on the lawn!"

"You could if Lady Warburton choked on the soup."

Isobel smiled wanly. "You're right," she agreed. "I could."

But dinner was a nightmare. Aside from Omegus, no one greeted Isobel. It was as if they had not seen her, even though she came down the great staircase, dark satins rustling, and the outswept edge of her skirts actually brushed those of Blanche Twyford because she did not move to allow her past. A moment later, as Vespasia passed, Blanche stepped aside graciously.

The conversation was free-flowing, but Isobel was not included. She spoke once, but no one appeared to hear her.

When the butler announced that dinner was served, Omegus offered her his arm, because it was apparent that no other man was going to. Once they were seated, Lady Warburton looked at Lady Vespasia, then at Omegus.

"Am I mistaken, Mr. Jones, or did you lay down the rules of this medieval trial of yours with the intention that we were all to be bound by them or our own honor was also forfeit?"

"I did, Lady Warburton," he replied.

"Then perhaps you would explain them to me again. You seem to be flouting what I understood you to say." She looked meaningfully at Isobel, then back again at Omegus with a wide challenging gaze.

He colored faintly. "You are right, Lady Warburton," he conceded. "I am as bound as anyone else, but I am still hoping that Mrs. Alvie will reconsider her refusal, and then a final decision must be made. I choose to wait until then before I act."

"I suppose you have that privilege," she said grudgingly. "At least while we are at Applecross."

The meal began, and Isobel was served exactly as everyone else was, but when she requested that the salt be passed to her, Fenton Twyford, who was next to her, looked across the table at Peter Hanning and asked his opinion on the likely winner of the Derby next year.

"Would you be kind enough to pass me the salt?" Isobel reiterated.

"I must say I disagree," Twyford said loudly in the silence. "I think that colt of Bamburgh's will take it. What do you think, Rosythe?"

Isobel did not ask again.

The rest of the meal proceeded in the same way. She was ignored as if her seat were empty. People spoke of Christmas, and of next year, who would attend what function during the season — the balls, races, regattas, garden parties, exhibitions, the opera, the theater, the pleasure cruises down the Thames. No one asked Isobel where she was going. They behaved as if she would not be there. There was no grief as if for the dead, as when Gwendolen's name was mentioned. It was not simply a ceasing to be, but as if she had never been.

She remained at the table, growing paler and paler. Vespasia walked beside her when the ladies withdrew to leave the gentlemen to their port. It was painful to remember that this time yesterday Gwendolen had been with them. None of the tragedy had happened. Now she was lying in one of the unused morning rooms, and tomorrow the undertaker would come to dress her for the grave.

Perhaps it was the closeness of the hour to the event, but as the women entered the withdrawing room, each one fell silent. Vespasia found herself shivering. Death was not a stranger to any of them. There were many diseases, the risks of childbirth, the accidents of even quite ordinary travel, but this was different, and the darkness of it touched them all.

Within twenty minutes of the door closing, Isobel rose to her feet, and since they had not acknowledged her presence, she did not bother to excuse her leaving. She went out in silence.

Vespasia followed almost immediately. Not only did she need to see Isobel and try in every way she could to persuade her to make the journey to Scotland, she felt she could not bear to stay any longer in the withdrawing room with the other women and observe their gloating. There was something repellent in their relishing of Isobel's downfall and the doling out of punishment, because it had nothing to do with justice, or the possibility of expiation. It was to do with personal safety and the satisfaction of being one of the included, not of those exiled.

Vespasia went back across the hallway, where she was greeted courteously by the butler. She wished him good night, wondering how awkward it was going to be for the domestic staff to work their way through the silences and rebuffs and decide whose leads to follow. Perhaps the real question was, how long would Omegus hold out against his own edict?

At the top of the stairs she retraced her path along the east wing and knocked on Isobel's door.

Again it was not answered, and again she went in.

Isobel was standing in the middle of the floor, her body stiff, her face white with misery. "Don't you ever wait to be invited?" Her husky voice was on the edge of losing control.

Vespasia closed the door behind her. "I don't think I can afford to wait," she replied.

Isobel took a deep breath, steadying herself with a visible effort. "And what can you possibly say that matters?" she asked.

Vespasia swept her considerable skirt to one side and sat down on the bedroom chair, as if she intended to stay for some time. "Do you intend to accept virtual banishment? And don't delude yourself that it will only be by those who are here this weekend, because it will not. They will repeat it all as soon as they return to London. By next season all society will have one version of it or another. If you are honest, you know that is true."

Isobel's eyes swam with tears, but she refused to give way to them. "Are you going to suggest that I accept the blame for Gwendolen's death and take this wretched letter to her mother?" she said, her voice choking. "All I did was imply that she was ambitious, which was perfectly true. Most women are. We have to be."

"You were cruel, and funny at her expense." Vespasia added the further truth. "You implied she was ambitious, but also that her love for Bertie would cease to exist were he in a different social or financial class."

Isobel's dark eyes widened. "And you are claiming that it would not? You believe she would marry a greengrocer? Or a footman?"

"Of course not," Vespasia said impatiently. "To begin with, no greengrocer or footman would ask her. The point is irrelevant. Your remark was meant to crush her and make her appear greedy and, more important, to make Bertie see her love for him as merely opportunism. Don't be disingenuous, Isobel."

Isobel glared at her, but she was too close to losing control to trust herself to speak.

"Anyway," Vespasia went on briskly. "None of it matters very much —"

"Is that what you intruded into my bedroom to tell me?" Isobel gasped, the tears brimming over and running down her cheeks. "Get out! You are worse than they are! I imagined you were my friend, and, my God, how mistaken I was! You are a hypocrite!"

Vespasia remained exactly where

she was. She did not even move enough to rustle the silk of her gown. "What matters," she said steadily, "is that we face the situation as it is, and deal with it. None of them is interested in the truth, and it is unlikely we will ever know exactly why Gwendolen killed herself, far less prove it to people who do not wish to know. But Omegus has offered you a chance not only to expiate whatever guilt you might have, but to retain your position in society and oblige everyone here to keep absolute silence about it or face ostracism themselves — which is a feat of genius, I believe." She smiled slightly. "And if you succeed, you will have the pleasure of watching them next season, watching you and being unable to say a word. Lady Warburton and Blanche Twyford will find it extremely hard. They will suffer every moment of forced civility in silence. That alone should be of immeasurable satisfaction to you. It will be to me!"

Isobel smiled a little tremulously. She took a shuddering breath. "All the way to Inverness?"

"There will be trains," Vespasia responded. "The line goes that far now."

Isobel looked away. "That will be the least part of it. I daresay it will take days, and be cold and uncomfortable, with infinite stops. But facing that woman, and giving her Gwendolen's letter, which might say anything about me! And having to wait and watch her grief? It will be . . . unbearable!"

"It will be difficult, but not unbearable," Vespasia corrected.

Isobel stared at her furiously. "Would you do it? And don't you dare lie to me!"

Vespasia heard her own voice with amazement. "I will do. I'll come with you."

Isobel blinked. "Really? You promise?"

Vespasia breathed in and out slowly. What on earth had she committed herself to? She was not guilty of any offense toward Gwendolen Kilmuir. But had that really anything to do with it? Neither guilt nor innocence was really the issue. Friendship was — and need. "Yes," she said aloud. "I'll come with you. We shall set off tomorrow morning. We will have to go to London first, of course, and then take the next train to Scotland. We will deliver the letter to Mrs. Naylor, and we will accompany her back here if she will allow us to. Omegus said nothing about your journeying alone — merely that you had to go."

"Thank you," Isobel said, the tears running unchecked down her face. "Thank you very much."

Vespasia stood up. "We shall tell them tomorrow morning at breakfast. Have your maid pack, and dress for traveling. Wear your warmest suit and your best boots. There will probably be snow farther north, and it will be bound to be colder."

Vespasia's mind whirled with the enormity of her decision. When she finally fell asleep, her dreams were of roaring trains and windy snowswept landscapes, and a grief-stricken and unforgiving woman bereft of her child.

She woke with a headache, dressed for travel, and left her maid packing while she went down to breakfast.

Everyone was assembled, ready to begin the new day's ostracism. The dining room was warm, the fire lit, and the sideboard laden with silver dishes from which delicious aromas emanated. Only Omegus looked distinctly unhappy. Almost immediately he caught Vespasia's eye, and she smiled at him, giving an imperceptible nod, and she saw the answering flash of light in his eyes. His body eased, and his right hand unclenched where it lay on the fresh linen of the table.

Isobel came in almost on Vespasia's heels, as if she had been waiting.

Everyone greeted Vespasia as effusively as they calculatedly ignored Isobel. This time she did not speak, but took her place at the table with a calm, pale face and began to eat after helping herself from the toast rack and the teapot.

Peter Hanning mentioned the weather and invited Bertie to a game of billiards in the afternoon. Lord Salchester announced that he was going for a walk. Lady Salchester said that she would accompany him, which took the smile from his face.

Isobel finished her toast and stood up, turning to Omegus.

"Mr. Jones, I have given your offer much serious thought. I was mistaken to refuse it. A chance to redeem oneself, and have past errors forgotten as if they had not existed, is something given far too rarely, and should not be declined. I shall leave Applecross this morning, taking the letter to Mrs. Naylor with me, and I shall catch the first available train to Scotland and deliver it to her. If she will accept my company on the return, then I shall do that also. When we reach London again, I shall inform you of the outcome, and trust that everyone here will keep their word according to our bond."

Lady Warburton looked crestfallen, as if she had lifted a particularly delicate morsel to her lips, only to have it fall onto the floor.

The ghost of a smile touched Isobel's face.

"How shall we know that you gave

the letter to Mrs. Naylor, and did not merely say that you did?" Lady Warburton asked irritably.

"You will have Mrs. Alvie's word for it!" Omegus answered coldly.

"You will also have Mrs. Naylor's word, should you wish to ask her," Isobel pointed out.

"Really!" Lady Warburton subsided into indignant silence.

"Bravo," Lord Salchester said softly. "You have courage, my dear. It will not be a comfortable journey."

"It will be abysmal!" Fenton Twyford added. "Inverness could be knee-deep in snow, and the shortest day of the year is only three weeks away. In the far north of Scotland that could mean hardly any daylight at all. You do realize Inverness is another hundred and fifty miles north of

Edinburgh, I suppose. At least!"

"What if your train gets stuck in a snowdrift?" Blanche asked hopefully.

"It is the beginning of December, not mid-January," Sir John Warburton pointed out. "It could be perfectly pleasant. Inverness-shire is a fine county."

Lady Warburton looked surprised. "When were you ever there?"

He smiled. "Oh, once or twice. So was Fenton, you know."

"Doing what?"

"Wonderful country for walking."

"In December?" Hanning's eyebrows shot up, and his voice was sharp with disbelief.

"It hardly matters," Vespasia interrupted. "Now is when we are going. We shall leave as soon as our packing is completed — if the trap can be arranged to take us to the railway station."

"You are leaving, as well?" Lord Salchester said with clear disappointment.

Omegus looked at Vespasia.

"Yes," she replied.

Isobel smiled, pride in her face, and a shadow of uncertainty. "Lady Vespasia has offered to come with me."

Omegus smiled, a sweet, shining look that lit his face, making him beautiful.

"To give the letter to Mrs. Naylor, if Mrs. Alvie should lose her nerve?" Blanche Twyford said bitingly. "That hardly makes of it the ordeal it is supposed to be!" She turned to Omegus. "Are we still bound by our oaths, in spite of this new turn of events?"

Omegus turned to her. "In the medieval trials of which I spoke, and upon which I have modeled my plan, the accused person was permitted friends to speak for them, and the friend risked facing the sure punishment along with them. If found guilty, the accused person promised to undertake the pilgrimage assigned, and if their friend were sure enough of their worth, had the courage and the selflessness to go with them, then that was the greatest mark of friendship that they could show. Neither the physical hardship nor the spiritual journey will be lessened, nor the threats that face them along the way. They will simply face them together, rather than alone. And the answer to your question, Mrs. Twyford, is, yes, you are just as bound."

Lord Salchester looked at Vespasia. "Remarkable," he said with very obvious admiration. "I admire your loyalty, my dear."

"Stubbornness," Lady Warburton said under her breath.

Bertie avoided eye contact with Isobel.

Vespasia looked at Omegus, who was regarding her with a happiness that she found suddenly and startlingly disconcerting. She wondered for a moment if she had made the rash promise for Isobel's sake, or just so she could see that look in Omegus's eyes. Then she dismissed it as absurd and finished her breakfast.

The ladies' maids would follow

later with their luggage and remain at their respective houses in London. The expiatory journey was to be made alone. It would be both unfair and compromising to the integrity of the oath were the maids to have gone, as well. They did not deserve the hardship; nor were they party to any agreement of silence.

Vespasia and Isobel departed just after ten o'clock, with ample time to catch the next train to London. Omegus saw them off at the front door, his hair whipped by the fresh, hard wind that blew off the sweeping parkland with the clean smell of rain.

"I shall be waiting for your word from London," he said quietly. "I wish you Godspeed."

"Are you quite sure it is acceptable for Vespasia to come with me? I have no intention of making this journey only to discover at the end that it doesn't count."

"It counts," he assured her. "Do not underestimate the difficulties ahead, just because you are not alone. Vespasia may ease some of it for you, both by her presence and her wit and courage, but it is you who must face Mrs. Naylor. Should she do that for you, then indeed you will not have made your expiation. If you should lie, society may forgive you, unable to prove your deceit, but you will know, and that is what matters in the end."

"I won't lie!" Isobel said stiffly, anger tight in her voice.

"Of course you will not," he agreed. "And Vespasia will be your witness, in case Mrs. Naylor is not inclined to be."

Isobel bit her lip. "I admit, I had not thought of that. I suppose it would not be surprising. I . . . I wish I knew what that letter said!"

His face shadowed. "You cannot," he said with a note of warning. "I am afraid that uncertainty is part of your journey. Now you must go, or you may miss the train. It is a long wait until the next one." He turned to Vespasia. "Much will happen to you before I see you again, my dear. Please God, the harvest of it will be good. Godspeed."

"Good-bye, Omegus," she answered, accepting his hand to climb up into the trap and seat herself with the rug wrapped around her knees.

The groom urged the pony forward as Isobel clasped her hands in front of her, staring ahead into the wind, and

Vespasia turned once to see Omegus still standing in the doorway, a slender figure, arms by his sides, but still watching them until they went around the corner of the driveway and the great elm tree trunks closed him from sight.

Part Two

The train journey to London seemed tedious, but it was in fact very short, little more than two hours, compared with the forthcoming journey northward. In London they took separate hansoms to their individual houses in order to pack more suitable clothes for the next step. Evening gowns would not be needed, and there would be no ladies' maids to care for them. Additional winter skirts and heavier jackets, boots, and capes were definite requisites.

Isobel and Vespasia agreed to meet at Euston Station preparatory to catch the northbound train at five o'clock that afternoon. Vespasia arrived first, and was angry with herself for being anxious in case Isobel at the last moment lost her nerve. She paced back and forth on the freezing platform. Odd how railway stations always seemed to funnel the wind until it increased its strength and its biting edge to twice whatever it was anywhere else! And of course, the air was full of steam, flying smuts of soot, and the noise — shouting, doors clanging to, and people coming and going.

Then fifteen minutes before the train was due to depart, she saw Isobel's tall figure sweeping ahead of a porter with her baggage, her head jerking from right to left as she searched for Vespasia, obviously afflicted by the same fear of facing the journey, and its more dreadful arrival, alone.

"Thank heaven!" she said, her voice shaking with intense relief as she saw Vespasia. She waved her arm at the porter. "Thank you! This will be excellent. Please put them aboard for me." And she opened her reticule to find an appropriate reward for him.

"Did you doubt me?" Vespasia asked her.

"Of course not!" Isobel said with feeling. "Did you doubt me?"

"Of course not!" Vespasia replied, smiling.

"Liar!" Isobel smiled back. "It's going to be awful, isn't it!" It was not a question.

"I should think so," Vespasia agreed. "Do you wish to turn back?"

Isobel pulled a rueful face, and there was honesty and fear in her eyes. "I would love to, but it would be worse in the end. Besides, I told those wretched people that I would. I sealed my fate then. Nothing this could do to me would be worse than facing them if I fail!"

"Of course. That was the whole purpose of saying it at the breakfast table, surely?" Vespasia stopped the porter and added her financial appreciation as he loaded her luggage, as well, just one case, more and warmer clothes, in case they should be needed. If they were fortunate, the whole mission could be accomplished in two days, and they would be able to return. The long weekend at Applecross would be barely finished before they were in London again.

The train pulled out with whistles

and clangs and much belching of steam. Slowly it picked up speed through the city, past serried rows of rooftops, then green spaces, factories, more houses, and eventually out into the open countryside, now patched with the dark turned earth of plowed fields and the scattered leafless copses of woodland. The rhythm of the wheels over the track would have been soothing, were they going anywhere else.

The winter afternoon faded quickly, and it was not more than an hour before they were rushing through the night, the steam past the window reduced to the red lines from lit sparks at speed, everything else a blur of darkness.

They stopped regularly, to set down passengers or to pick up more, and, of course, to allow people to stretch their legs, avail themselves of necessary facilities, and purchase refreshments of one sort or another.

Vespasia tried to sleep through as much of the night as she could. The movement of the train was pleasant and kept up a steady kind of music, but sitting more or less upright was far from comfortable. She was aware of Isobel watching the lights of stations and towns pass by with their steady progress northward, and knew she must dread their arrival. But they had exhausted discussion of the subject and Vespasia declined to be drawn into speculation any further.

Dawn came gray and windswept as they climbed beyond the Yorkshire moors to the bleaker and more barren heights of Durham, and then

Northumberland, and at last on toward the border with Scotland. They purchased breakfast at one of the many stations and took it back to eat on the train as it pulled out again.

Vespasia determined not to return to the reason for their visit and talked instead of subjects that might ordinarily have aroused their interest — fashion, theater, gossip, political events. Neither of them cared just now, but Isobel joined in the fiction that everything was as usual.

As they crossed the Lowlands toward Edinburgh, the brooding and magnificent city that was Scotland's capital and seat of power and learning, the skies cleared, and it was merely briskly cold. They alighted and, with the help of a porter, took their luggage to await the train for the last hundred and fifty miles to Inverness.

An hour and a half later they were aboard, stiff, cold, and extremely tired, but again moving northward. As they came into Stirlingshire there was snow on the hills, but the black crown of Stirling Castle stood out against a blue sky with windragged clouds streaming across it like banners.

The country grew wilder. The slopes were black with faded heather and the peaks higher and brilliant white against the sky. On the lower slopes they saw herds of red deer, and once what looked like an eagle, a dark spot circling in the sky, but it could have been a buzzard. The early afternoon was fading when at last they pulled into Inverness and saw the sprawl of sunset fire across the south, its light reflected paler on the sea. The mound of the Black Isle lay to the north, and beyond that, snow-gleaming mountains of Ross-shire and Sutherland.

The wind on the platform was like a scythe, cutting through even the best woolen clothing, and there was the smell of snow in it, and vast, clean spaces. It was an unconscious decision to find lodgings for the night rather than make any attempt to find Mrs. Naylor's house in the dark, in a town with which neither of them had the slightest familiarity. The station hotel seemed to offer excellent rooms, and had two available. The morning was soon enough to face the ultimate test.

Inquiry of the staff of the hotel elicited the information that the address on Gwendolen's letter was not actually in Inverness itself but was a considerable estate on the outskirts of Muir-of-Ord, a town some distance away, for which it would be necessary to hire a trap, and it would take a good part of the morning to reach it.

Thus it was actually close to midday when they finally reached the Naylor house, set on several acres of richly wooded land sweeping down to the Beauly Firth and ultimately the open sea.

Vespasia looked at Isobel. "Are you ready?" she asked gently.

"No, nor will I ever be," Isobel responded. "But then, I am so cold I am not even sure if I can stand on my feet, and whatever lies within that house, it cannot be less comfortable than sitting out here."

Vespasia wished profoundly that that would prove to be true, but she did not say so aloud.

They alighted, thanked the driver, and asked him to wait, in case they should not be invited to remain and have no way of returning to the town. Vespasia hung back and allowed Isobel to step forward and pull the bell knob beside the door. She was about to reach for it a second time, impatient to get the ordeal over, when it swung open and an elderly manservant looked at her inquiringly.

"Good morning," Isobel said, her voice catching with nervousness now that the moment was upon her. "My name is Isobel Alvie. I have come from London with a letter of importance to give to Mrs. Naylor. With me is my friend Lady Vespasia Cumming-Gould. I would be most grateful if you could give Mrs. Naylor that message, and apologize for my not having sent my card first, but the journey is urgent, and was unexpected." She offered him her card now.

"If you will come in, Mrs. Alvie, Lady Vespasia, I shall consider what is best to do," the man said in a soft northern accent.

Isobel hesitated. "What is best to do?" she repeated.

"Aye, madame. Mrs. Naylor is not at home, but I am sure she would wish you to receive the hospitality of the house. Please come in." He held the door wide for them.

Isobel glanced at Vespasia, then with a shrug so slight it was barely visible, she followed the manservant over the step and inside. Vespasia went after her into a large low-beamed hall with a fire blazing in an open hearth, then past it and into an informal sitting room with sunlight vivid through windows. A lawn sloped downward to a magnificent view beyond, but it was distinctly cooler.

"When do you expect Mrs. Naylor?" Isobel inquired. Her voice was rough-edged, and Vespasia could hear the tension in it.

"I'm sorry, madame, but I have no idea," the man said gravely. "I'm sorry you've traveled all this way an' we cannot help you."

"Where has she gone?" Isobel asked. "You must know!"

He looked startled at her persistence. It was discourteous, to say the least.

Vespasia stepped forward. She was not completing the task for Isobel, only ensuring that she had the opportunity to do it for herself. "I apologize if we seem intrusive," she said gently. "But there has been a tragedy in London, and it concerns Mrs. Naylor's daughter. We have to bring her news of it, no matter how difficult that may be. Please understand our distress and concern."

"Miss Gwendolen?" The man's face pinched with some emotion of pain, but it was impossible to read in it more than that. "Poor bairn," he said sadly. "Poor bairn."

"We must tell Mrs. Naylor," Vespasia said again. "And deliver the letter into her hands. It is a duty we have given our word to complete."

The man shook his head. "It's no another death, is it?" he asked, looking from one to the other of them, and back again.

Vespasia allowed Isobel to answer.

"Yes, I am terribly sorry to tell you, it is. So you see why we must speak to Mrs. Naylor in person. We were both there, and can at least tell her something of it, if she should wish to know."

"It'll be Miss Gwendolen herself this time," he said, shaking his head stiffly, his eyes bright and far distant.

Vespasia felt intrusive in his shock and sadness.

"Yes. I'm profoundly sorry," Isobel answered. "Where can we find her, or send a message so she may return, if that is what she would prefer? We are prepared to accompany her south, if she would permit us to."

"Aye, mebbe." He nodded awkwardly. "Mebbe. It's a long journey, and that's the truth."

"Yes, it is, but the train transfer in Edinburgh is not too inconvenient."

"Oh, lassie, there's no train from Ballachulish, and no likely to be in your lifetime, or your grandbairns', neither," he said with a sad little smile. "And mebbe that's for the best, too. Boat to Glasgow, it'll be. I've heard tell there's railways to Glasgow now." He spoke of it with an expression as if it were some exotic and far-distant Babylon.

"Ballachulish?" Isobel repeated uncertainly. "Where is that? How does one get there?"

"Oh, to Inverness, it'll be," he replied. "And then down the loch to the Caledonian Canal, and mebbe Fort William. Or else across Rannoch Moor and through Glencoe. Balla-chulish lies at the end of it, so I'm told."

"How far is it?" Isobel obviously had no idea at all.

"Lassie, it's the other side o' Scot-land! On the west coast, it is."

Isobel took a deep breath. "When will Mrs. Naylor be back?"

"That's it, you see," he said, shaking his head. "She won't, least not so far as we know. It might be next spring, or then again it might not."

Isobel was horrified. "But that's . . . that's the other side of winter!"

"Aye, so it is. You're welcome to stay the night, while you think on it," he offered. "There's plenty of room. There's been barely a soul in the house since poor Mr. Kilmuir met his accident. It'll be good to have someone to cook for, and the sound of voices not our own."

"Has Mrs. Naylor been gone so long?" Vespasia put in with surprise. "I thought that was well over a year ago."

"Year and a half," he replied. "Early summer, it was, of '51. Now, if I can get you some luncheon, perhaps? You'll not have eaten, I'll be bound."

"Thank you," Vespasia accepted before Isobel could demur. They needed sustenance, and even more they needed the time it would take in order to make a decision in the face of this devastating news.

"What on earth are we going to do?" Isobel asked as soon as they were alone in the main hall again where the fire was warmer. "Will they listen if I explain to them that Mrs. Naylor wasn't here, and wherever she is, is at the other side of Scotland, and there's no way to get there?"

"No," Vespasia said frankly. "For a start, if she is there, then there must be a way for us to get there, also." But as she said it she felt panic well up inside her. She had spoken on impulse when she promised to come as far as Inverness with Isobel. Part of it was sympathy, part a profound and increasing dislike for Lady Warburton and a desire to see her thwarted, and a good deal more than she had realized before, a desire for Omegus's respect, even admiration. Now it was beginning to look like a far greater task than she had bargained for. But pride would not let her falter now, and honesty would not allow her to let Isobel believe that what they had done so far would satisfy their oath.

Isobel stared into the fire, her face set, jaw tight. "This is ridiculous! Why on earth did this wretched woman go across to the other side of the country? How did Gwendolen suppose anyone was going to get a letter to her? Nobody thought about that when they sent us on a wild-goose chase all the way up here!"

It was an implied criticism of Omegus, and Vespasia found it stung.

"Nobody sent us here," she replied. "It was an opportunity offered so you could redeem yourself from a stupid

142

and cruel remark which ended in tragedy. Omegus did not cause any part of that."

Isobel swung around in her chair. "If Gwendolen had any courage at all, she would simply have answered me back! Not gone off and thrown herself into the lake! Or if she wanted to make a grand gesture, then she could at least have done it in the daytime, when someone would have seen her and pulled her out!"

"Sodden wet, her clothes clinging to her, her hair like rats' tails, covered in mud and weed? To do what, for heaven's sake?" Vespasia asked. "It may be romantic to fling yourself into the lake. It is merely ridiculous to be dragged out of it!" But as she stood up and walked away from Isobel toward the window looking over the long slope toward the sea, other thoughts stirred in her mind, memories of Gwendolen happy and with ever-growing confidence. Deliberately she then pictured the moment Isobel had spoken, the freezing seconds before anything had changed, and then Gwendolen's face stricken with horror. She did not understand it. It was out of proportion to the cruelty of the words. That Bertie did not defend her and then later did not even go after her to protest his disbelief of anything so shallow in her must have hurt her more than she could bear; it was the wound of disillusion. Perhaps she really had loved him and not seen his reality before.

She tried to recall Gwendolen all through the season. Had she really seemed so fragile? Image after image came to her mind. They were all ordinary, a young woman emerging from mourning, beginning to enjoy herself again, laughing, flirting a little, being careful with expenses, but not seemingly in any difficulty. But had Vespasia looked at her more than superficially?

For that matter, had she looked at Isobel more than as an intelligent companion, a little different from the ordinary, with whom it was agreeable to spend time, because she had opinions and did not merely say what was expected of her? Vespasia had not honestly sought anything more from her than a relief from tedium. She had told Isobel nothing of herself, certainly nothing of Rome. But she had told nobody of that.

How odd that Mrs. Naylor had left

here so soon after Kilmuir's death, and apparently with no intention of returning. Something must have prompted such an extraordinary decision.

She turned and walked out of the hall into the corridor and along to the doorway at the end, which opened onto a gravel path. It was a bright day with a chill wind blowing off the water. The garden was beautifully kept, with grass smooth as a bowling green, perennial flowers clipped back, fruit trees carefully espaliered against the south-facing walls. She walked until she found a man coming from the kitchen garden, and complimented him on it. He thanked her solemnly.

"Mrs. Naylor must miss this very much," she said conversationally. "Is

Ballachulish equally pleasant?"

"Och, it's very grand, and all that, with the mountains and the glen, and so on," he answered. "But the west is too wet for my liking. It's a land full of moods. Very dramatic. No much use for growing a garden like this."

"Why would one choose to live there?" How bold dare she be?

"There you have me, my lady," he confessed. "I couldn' a do it, and that's the truth. But if you're a west-coaster, it's different. They love it like it was woven into their skins."

"Oh? Mrs. Naylor is a west-coaster?" How simple after all.

"Not she! She's an Englishwoman like yourself," he said as if it surprised him, too. "She just took up and went there after poor Mr. Kilmuir was killed. Took it terrible hard. Mind, it was a bad thing, and so sudden, poor man."

"Yes, indeed," she said sympathetically, shivering a little as the wind knifed in over the water, ruffled and white-crested now. "Although I never heard exactly what happened. Poor Gwendolen was too shocked to speak of it."

"Horse bolted," he said, lowering his voice. "Kilmuir and Mrs. Naylor were out in the trap. He was thrown over by a branch, and got himself caught in the rein by his wrist."

"He was dragged?" she said in horror. "How appalling! No wonder Gwendolen could not speak of it! Poor Mrs. Naylor. She must have been frightened half out of her wits!"

"Och, no, madame, not she!" he said briskly, dismissing the very idea.

"You do not know Mrs. Naylor if you could think that! More courage than any man I know! Any two men!" He lifted his head with fierce pride as he said it. He looked at her through furrowed brows. "You can smile, but it's true! Stopped the horse herself, but too late to help him, of course. Must have gone in the first moments. Cut the animal free and rode it home to tell us. Clear as day it was, when we found the wreckage, and poor Kilmuir."

"And Mrs. Kilmuir?" she asked.

He shook his head. "That's the worst of it, madame. She was out riding, and she saw the whole thing, but too far away to do anything but watch, like seeing your life coming to an end in front of your eyes." He shook his head minutely. "Didn't think she'd ever be the same again, poor child. Inconsolable, she was. Wandered around like a ghost, didn't eat a morsel, nor say a word to anyone. Glad we were when she finally went back to London, and word came that she'd started her life again, the poor lass."

"And Mrs. Naylor didn't go with her?"

His face stiffened and something within him closed. "No. She's no fondness for London, and too much to do up here. And if you'll be excusing me, my lady, I have to take these in for Cook to prepare dinner, since you and your friend will be staying. We'd like to treat you to our best, seeing as you're friends of Mrs. Kilmuir's. Walk in the garden all you will, and welcome."

She thanked him and continued on, but her mind was lost in picturing the death of Kilmuir, Mrs. Naylor's reaction, and her attempts to comfort a shattered daughter who had accidentally witnessed it all. She felt a consuming guilt that now they had to find Mrs. Naylor and tell her even worse news. The question of returning to London and simply leaving Gwendolen's letter to be found when she returned, whenever that was, had been irrevocably answered. It was unthinkable.

She told Isobel so when they were alone after dinner.

Isobel turned from the window where she had been standing before the open curtains, staring at the darkness and the water beyond. "Go down the Caledonian Canal, and then overland to Balla . . . whatever it is," she said in anguish. "How would we do that? Would anyone in their right mind at this time of year? Apart from sheepherders and brigands, that is!"

"Well, I shall try it," Vespasia responded. "If you wish to go back to London, then I am sure they will take you to Inverness. I shall go on at least as far as I can, and attempt to deliver the letter to Mrs. Naylor and tell her as much as I know of what happened."

Isobel's face was white, her eyes wide and angry. "That is moral blackmail!" she accused bitterly. "You know what they would say if I went back when you went on! It would be even worse for me than if I'd never come!"

"Yes, it probably would," Vespasia agreed. "So you will blackmail me into going back and leaving that poor woman to discover that her daughter is dead — whenever she returns here, this year, or next!"

Isobel blinked.

"We appear to have reached an impasse," Vespasia observed coolly. "Perhaps we should both do as we think right? I am going to Ballachulish, or as far toward it as I can. As you may have noticed, there is very little snow so far."

Isobel bit her lip and turned away. "You always get what you want, don't you?" she said quietly. Her voice was trembling, but it was impossible to tell if it was from anger or fear. "You have money, beauty, and a title, and by heaven, do you know how to use them!" And without looking back she swept out of the room, and Vespasia heard her steps across the hall.

Vespasia stood alone. Surely what Isobel said was not true? Was she so spoiled, so protected from the reality of other people's lives? Certainly she had great beauty; she could hardly fail to be aware of that. If the looking glass had not told her, then the envy of women and the adoration of men would have. It was fun; of course it was. But what was it worth? In a few years it would fade, and those who valued her for that alone would leave her for the new beauty of the day — younger, fresher.

And, yes, she had money. She admitted she was unfamiliar with want for any material thing. And a title?

That, too. It opened all manner of doors that would always be closed to others. Was she spoiled? Was she without any true imagination or compassion? Did she lack strength, because she had never been tested?

No, that was not true! Rome had tested her to the last ounce of her strength. Isobel would never know what she would have given to stay there with Mario, whatever their ideological differences, his republicanism and her monarchist loyalty, his revolutionary passion and fire and her belief in treasuring old and beautiful ways that had proved good down the centuries. Over it all towered his laughter, his warmth, his courage to live or die for his beliefs. How unlike the ordinary, pedestrian kindness of her husband, who gave her freedom but left her soul empty.

However, that was nothing to do with Isobel, and she would never know of it. This was her journey of expiation, not Vespasia's.

They set out immediately after breakfast, Mrs. Naylor's household providing them with transport by pony and trap as far as Inverness and then beyond to the eastern end of Loch Ness, where they could hire a boat. It would take them the length of the long, winding inland lake with its steep mountainsides as if it were actually a great cleft in the earth filled with fathomless satin gray water, bright as steel. All the way there they had spoken barely a word to each other, sitting side by side in the trap, the wind in their faces, rugs wrapped tightly around their knees.

"It's a good thirty mile to Fort Augustus, so it is," the boatman said as they embarked. He shook his head at the thought. "Then there's the canal, and another good thirty mile o' that, before you reach Fort William on the coast." He squinted up at the sky. "And they always say in the west that if you can see the hills, it'll rain as sure as can be."

"And if you can't?" Isobel asked.

"Then it's raining already." He smiled.

"Then we'd best get started," she answered briskly. "Since it is a fine day now, obviously it is going to rain!"

"Aye," he acknowledged. "If that's what you want?"

Without looking at Vespasia, Isobel repeated that it was, and accepted the boatman's assistance into the stern of the small vessel, most of it open to the elements. It was the only way in which they could begin their journey.

They pulled out into the open water, but stayed closer to the northern shore, as if the center might hold promise of sudden storm, and indeed several times squalls appeared out of nowhere. One moment everything was dazzling with silver light on the water, the slopes of the mountains vivid greens. Then out of the air came a darkness, the peaks were shrouded, and the distance veiled over with impenetrable sheets of driving rain.

They sheltered in the tiny cabin as the boat rocked and swung, flinging them from side to side. They said nothing, so cold their limbs shook, teeth clenched together. Vespasia cursed her own pride for coming, Isobel for her cruel tongue, Omegus for his redeeming ideas, and Gwendolen for wanting a shallow man like Bertie Rosythe and falling to pieces when she realized what he was.

"Do you suppose Gwendolen was still in love with Kilmuir?" Vespasia asked when they finally emerged into a glittering world, the water a flat mirror, burning with light in the center, mountains dark as basalt above, and drifts of rain obscuring in the distance.

Isobel looked at her in surprise. "You mean she realized it that evening, and the grief of losing him returned to her?" There was a lift of hope in her voice.

"Did you know her, other than just socially during the season?" Vespasia questioned.

Isobel thought for a few moments. They passed a castle on the foreshore, its outline dramatic against the mountains behind. "A little," she answered. "I know there was a sadness in her under the gaiety on the surface. But then she was a widow. I know what that is like. Whether you loved your husband wildly or not, there is a terrible loneliness at times."

Vespasia felt a stab of guilt. "Of course there must be," she said gently. It was not Isobel's right to know that it afflicted her, also — a different kind of loneliness, a hunger that had never been fed, except in brief, dangerous moments, a shared cause, a time that could never have lasted.

"Actually I thought Kilmuir was a bit of a cad," Isobel went on thoughtfully. "I'm not sure that he was any better than Bertie Rosythe, really. But it's natural to remember only what was good about someone after they are dead."

Vespasia studied Isobel's face and saw doubt in it and something that looked like guilt as she stared across the bright water with its shifting patterns, and not once after that did she look back at Vespasia, nor raise the subject again.

They stayed the night ashore, and continued the next day, reaching Fort Augustus by evening. They parted from that boat and set out on the canal at sunrise in another. The biting cold, the sense of claustrophobia on the long, narrow boat, and the knowledge that they were moving ever farther from land familiar to them, even by repute, eased some of the tension between them.

But above all was the dread of meeting Mrs. Naylor and having to tell her the truth. They spoke, to break the silence of the vast land and the strangeness of the situation. They sat closer to each other to keep a little warmth, and they shared food when it was offered them, and laughed self-consciously at the inconvenience of the requirements of nature. They filled the long tedium of waiting for locks to fill or empty, stretching their legs by walking back and forth in the bitter wind, staring at the white-crowned hills.

Some time after dark on the fourth day from Inverness they arrived in Fort William, and again found lodgings. They were shivering with cold and exhaustion, and wretched beyond even thinking of how to move on from there to Ballachulish. They huddled by the fire, trying to get warm enough to think of sleep.

"Why, in the name of heaven, would Mrs. Naylor come here at all?" Isobel said wretchedly, rubbing her hands together and holding them out before the flames. "Let alone stay for a year and a half? No wonder Gwendolen never mentioned her. She was probably terrified in case anyone discovered she was insane!"

"Did she never mention her?" Vespasia asked, although Isobel's remark was sensible enough. She had wondered herself why Mrs. Naylor was not living in her very attractive house at Muir-of-Ord. If one wished seclusion, that was surely far enough from most society.

"Never," Isobel said frankly. "Which you must admit is unusual."

A new realization came to Vespasia. She had not appreciated before that Isobel had known Gwendolen so well that such an omission would be noticeable to her. In fact, there was rather a lot that Isobel had not said, but perhaps her own desire for Bertie Rosythe's affection was deeper than it had seemed at Applecross.

"Yes," Vespasia said aloud. "Yes, it is." Actually she wondered why Mrs. Naylor had not come to London with Gwendolen to chaperone her and give all the help she could in gaining a second husband as soon as it was decent to do so.

"Exactly." Isobel tried to move her chair even closer to the fire, then realized that it would place her feet practically in the hearth, and her skirts where a spark might catch them, and changed her mind. "I'm dreading meeting this woman." She looked up at Vespasia candidly. "Do you suppose she might actually be dangerous?"

Vespasia weighed in her mind the need to continue their journey to the end, wherever that might be, and her growing hunger to know the truth of Gwendolen's reason for taking her own life. She was becoming concerned that what they had seen at Applecross was only a small part of it. The more she considered it, the less did it seem a sufficient reason.

"I suppose it is possible," she answered. "What did Gwendolen say about her family, if she did not speak of her mother at all?"

"Very little. It was all Kilmuir, and I suppose even that was only how much she missed him." Isobel frowned. "Naturally, she did not speak of the event of his death, but one would not expect her to. It would have been in very poor taste, distressing for her and embarrassing for everyone else." She shivered again and wrapped her cloak more tightly around her shoulders. "I have to confess, she behaved as I think I would have myself in that. I cannot fault her. It is simply odd that with a mother still living she never referred to her at all. However, if she's quite deranged, it would explain it completely." She puckered her brow. "Do we really have to continue until we find her?"

"Do you wish to turn back?"

Isobel pulled a rueful little face. "I wished to turn back as soon as we left Applecross, but not nearly as much as I do now. But I suppose since we have come this far, I should hate to have it all be in vain." She smiled and her eyes were bright for a second. "When it gets unbearably cold, miserable, and far from anything even remotely like home, I think of how furious Lady Warburton and Blanche Twyford will be if I complete this and they are obliged to forgive me, and it gives me courage to go on."

Vespasia knew exactly what she meant. The thought of Lady Warburton being charming because she had no choice had warmed her frozen body and put new vigor in her step more than once.

She smiled. "What was he like, Kilmuir?"

Isobel turned away, a shadow falling between her and Vespasia again, as clearly as if it had been visible. "I don't know."

"Yes, you do," Vespasia insisted. "You knew Gwendolen far longer, and far better, than you have allowed me to suppose."

Isobel stared at her, her dark eyes wide and challenging. "If I did, why is that your concern? I am going to do my penance. Is that not enough for you? You, of all people, can see what a bitter thing it is!" She took a sudden sharp breath. "Is that actually why you are here, to make sure I do it all?

Is that why Omegus Jones sent you?"

Vespasia was taken aback. The accusation was so unjust it caught her completely by surprise. "I came because I thought the journey could be long and hard, possibly even dangerous, and the ending of it the most difficult of all, and that you might surely need a friend," she answered. "Had I been making it, I should not have wished to do it alone. And Omegus did not send me."

Shame filled Isobel's face. "I'm sorry," she said huskily. "I have not ever been that sort of a friend to anyone. I find it hard to believe you could do it for me. Why should you? I . . . I don't think I would do it for you." She looked away. "Not that you would ever need it, of course."

Vespasia was tempted to answer

her with truth, even to tell her some of the weight she carried within her, which was not only loneliness but, if she were honest, guilt as well, and fear. She had buried her memories of Rome, of passion, of the inner joy of not being alone in her dreams. Deliberately she had forced herself not to think of talking with someone who understood her words even before she said them, who filled one hunger even as he awoke others. She had refused to look at remembrance of the exhilaration of fighting with all her time and strength for a cause she believed in. She had returned to duty, to a round of social chitchat about a hundred things that did not matter and never had. She was now sitting with Isobel, whom she knew so little of, and who knew her even less, sharing the outward hardships of a journey, with an uncrossable gulf between them on the inner purpose of it; that she had no crusade anymore. She had no battle to fight except against boredom, and there was no victory at the end of it, only another day to fill with pastimes that nourished nothing inside her.

"You have no idea whether I would or not," she said quietly. "You know nothing about me, except what you see on the outside, and that is mostly whatever I wish you to see, as it is with all of us."

Isobel looked startled. It had never occurred to her that Vespasia was anything more than the perfect beauty she seemed.

The fire was burning low. The wind battered the rain against the glass and whined in the eaves. Unless it eased, the boat journey down the loch to Ballachulish was going to be rough and unpleasant, but at this time of the year it would be days if not weeks before there was another fine, still day. Waiting for it was not a choice.

Isobel seemed lost in thought, overcome by new, previously unimagined ideas.

"Why did you say what you did to Gwendolen?" Vespasia asked. "You half implied that her choice somehow lay between servants and gentlemen, and she chose gentlemen for reasons of money and ambition."

Isobel blushed. It was visible even in the dying firelight. It was several moments before she answered, and she did not look at Vespasia even then. "I know it was cruel," she said softly. "I suppose that's why I'm really making this ridiculous journey. Otherwise, when we got to Inverness and found Mrs. Naylor wasn't home, I might have posted the letter and said I had done my best." She gave a little shudder. "No — that's not true. I'm doing it because I know I won't survive in society if I don't, and I have nowhere else to go, nowhere else I know how to behave or what to do."

"The reason?" Vespasia prompted.

Isobel lifted one shoulder in half a shrug. "Gossip. Stupid, I expect, but I heard it in more than one place."

Vespasia waited. "That is only half an answer," she said at last.

Isobel chewed her lip. "Everyone turns a blind eye if a man beds a handsome parlor maid or two, as long as he is reasonably discreet about it.

A woman who was known to have slept with a footman would be ruined. She would be branded a whore. Her husband would disown her for it, and no one would blame him."

Vespasia could hardly believe it. "Are you saying Gwendolen Kilmuir slept with a footman? She must be insane! Far madder than her mother!"

Isobel looked at her at last. "No, I'm not saying she did, simply that there were rumors. Actually I think Kilmuir started them." She shut her eyes as if twisted by some deep, internal pain. "He was paying rather a lot of attention to Dolly Twyford, Fenton's youngest sister."

"I thought she wasn't married!" Vespasia was incredulous. There was a convention in certain circles: Once one had borne the appropriate children to one's husband, a married woman might then indulge her tastes, and as long as she did not behave with such indiscretion that it could not be overlooked, no one would chastise her for it. However, for a man to have an affair with a single woman was quite another thing. That would ruin her reputation and make any acceptable marriage impossible for her.

"She wasn't," Isobel agreed. "That was the whole point. The suggestion was that Gwendolen's conduct was so outrageous he would divorce her, and then after a suitable period, not very long, he would marry Dolly."

"Were they in love?"

"With what?" Isobel raised her eyebrows. "Dolly wanted a position in society, and the title probably coming to Kilmuir, and he wanted children.

He had been married to Gwendolen for six years, and there were none so far. He was growing impatient. At least, that was the gossip." Her voice dropped. "And I knew it."

Vespasia did not answer. To say that it did not matter would be a dishonesty that would serve no one. Some penance was due for such a cruelty, and they were both deeply aware of it. But more than that, her mind was racing over the new picture of Gwendolen as it emerged now. Had Bertie Rosythe heard the gossip, as well, and was that the truth of why he had not gone after her and reassured her of his love? Or worse than that, had he gone and, far from offering her any comfort, made it plain that he had no intentions toward her? Did she see herself as ruined, not only for him but for any marriage at all?

Or worse even than that, could such rumors be true? Which raised the bitterly ugly question of whether Kilmuir's death had been a highly fortunate accident for Gwendolen, releasing her from the possibility of a scandalous divorce, from which her reputation would never have recovered. Instead she had become a widow, with everyone's sympathy, and excellent prospects in time of marrying again. How fortunate for her that it had been Mrs. Naylor who had been with him in the carriage, and not Gwendolen herself.

They discussed it no more. The fire was fading, and sleep beckoned like comforting arms. They were both happy to go upstairs and sink into oblivion until the morning should require them to face the elements and attempt to reach Ballachulish.

It was a hard journey, even though not long as the crow or the gull were to fly. The sharp west wind obliged the little boat to tack back and forth down the coast through choppy seas, and both Isobel and Vespasia were relieved to put ashore at last in the tiny town of Ballachulish and feel the earth firm beneath their feet. They crossed the road from the harbor wall, heads down against the sleet, wind gusting, tearing skirts, and made their way to the inn. They asked the landlord about Mrs. Naylor, and his response brought them close to despair.

"Och, I'm that sorry to tell ye, but Mistress Naylor left Ballachulish nigh on a year ago!" he told them with chagrin.

"Left?" Isobel could scarcely believe it. "But she can't! Her household in Inverness told us she was here!"

"Aye, and so she was," he agreed, nodding. "But she left a year ago this Christmas. Grand lady, she was. Never knew any lady of such spirit, for all that she was as English as you are."

Isobel swallowed. "Where did she go? Do you know?"

"Aye, I do. Up through the Glen and over the moor to the Orchy. You'll no be going that way, though, till May or so. Even then it's a wild journey. Horses you'll need. The

179

High Road passes right around there, and then south."

Isobel looked at Vespasia, the first signs of defeat in her eyes.

Vespasia felt a rush of pity, first for Isobel, knowing what awaited her in London if she failed. They would not care what the reason was, or if they could or would have done differently themselves. They were looking for excuses, and any would serve. Then she felt for Mrs. Naylor. However mad she was, whatever reason had brought her here and then driven her to go up into Glencoe and beyond, she still deserved to be told about her daughter's death face-to-face, not in a letter half a year late.

"I accept that it may be difficult," she said to the landlord. "Is it possible, with good horses and a guide?"

The man considered for several seconds. "Aye," he said at last. "Ye'll be used to riding, I take it?" Vespasia looked at Isobel. She had no idea of the answer.

Isobel nodded. "Certainly. I've ridden in London often enough."

"Ye'll be needing a guide," he warned.

"Naturally," Vespasia agreed. "Would you arrange one for us, at whatever you consider a fair rate?"

Isobel blinked, but she made no demur.

So it was that the next morning they set out in the company of a grizzled man by the name of MacIan, with a strong Highland pony each to ride, and three more to follow with luggage, water, and food.

"Keep close!" MacIan warned, fixing them in turn with a skeptical eye. "I'll no have time to be nursemaiding ye, so if ye're in trouble, call out, don't just sit there and hope I'll be noticing, 'cause I won't. I've my work to keep these ponies on the track, not to speak of finding it mysel', if the weather turns." He cocked his head to one side and looked up at the wild sky with clouds racing across it casting the hills in brilliant light one moment, then shrouded in purple, and then black the next. The water in the loch was white-ruffled. The wind was laden with salt and the sharp smell of weed. It was ice-cold on the skin, whipping the blood up.

Isobel looked at Vespasia. For once

they understood each other perfectly. Pride kept them from turning back. "Of course," they both agreed, and when MacIan was satisfied that they meant it, they set out of the village on the rough road through ever-steepening mountains toward the great Glen of the most treacherous massacre in the history of Scotland. In the winter of 1692 the Campbell guests had risen in the night and slain their MacDonald hosts — man, woman, and child — all in the cause of loyalty to the Hanoverian king from the south.

They rode in silence, because no conversation was possible. The wind tore their breath away, even if the labor of riding in single file along the track and the grandeur of the scenery had not robbed them of the wish to frame words for it.

At about one o'clock they stopped for something to eat, but primarily to rest the ponies. They were slightly sheltered by a buttress of rock, and Vespasia leaned against it and stared around her. On every side jagged mountains soared into the sky. Some were dark with heather on the lower slopes, the peaks like white teeth in the giant, upturned skull of some vast creature left behind from the beginning of time. The smell of the snow whetted the edge of the wind. It was a land of golden eagles and red deer, pools of peat-dark water, avalanches, and blizzards. There was a majesty, a terror, and a beauty that burned itself into the soul.

They remounted and set off again, climbing higher as the valley rose and the sides became steeper yet. Darkness fell early, and they stopped at a small hut, almost invisible in the dusk, amid the rock outcrops. It offered little hospitality beyond shelter from the elements, both for them and for the ponies. Vespasia was glad of that. She would not have left any creature out in the storm that was threatening, let alone beasts upon whom their lives might depend.

"Mrs. Naylor must be a raving madwoman," Isobel said grimly, settling down to sleep in her clothes. The only concession to comfort was to take the pins out of her hair. "And I'm beginning to think we are, too."

Vespasia was obliged to agree with her. The longer this journey continued, the more concerned she became as to what manner of woman

Mrs. Naylor might be, and increasingly now, what had been the truth of the marriage between Gwendolen and Kilmuir, and exactly how he had died. Why had Gwendolen never spoken of her mother? What was the reason for what looked unmistakably like an estrangement?

Neither of them slept well. It was too cold and the wooden bunks were hard. It was a relief when daylight came and they could rise, eat a breakfast of oatmeal and salt, and drink hot tea, without milk, then continue on their way.

Outside was a staggering world. It had snowed during the night and the sky had cleared. The light was blinding. Sun glittered on ribbons of water cascading down the rock faces, hitting stones and leaping up, foaming white. An eagle drifted on the wind, a black speck against the blue.

They rode all day, resting only briefly for the ponies' sake. Vespasia was so tired from the unaccustomed exercise that every bone and muscle in her body ached, and she knew Isobel must feel the same, but neither of them would admit it. It was not that they imagined they were deceiving anyone, least of all MacIan; it was simply a matter of self-mastery. One complaint or admission would lead to another, and then perhaps thoughts of surrender. Once suggested, it would become a possibility, and that must not be permitted. The temptation was too powerful. Instead they concentrated on a few yards at a time, from here to the next turn in the track, the next stretch ahead.

Then just before dusk, as the sun was setting in shards of fire almost due south, the valley opened out and the great width of Rannoch Moor lay in front of them, dark-patched with heather and peat bogs, pools shining bronze in the dying light. In the distance of the sky, turquoise drifted into palest blue before the advancing shades of the night.

No one spoke, but Vespasia wondered if perhaps Mrs. Naylor were not so mad after all. This was a different kind of sanity, undreamed of in London.

They found shelter again, but it was bitterly cold, and by morning the aches that had been slight the previous day were now sharper and reminded them of pain with every movement. It required all the concentration Vespasia could muster just to stay on her pony and watch where she was going. Her head ached from clenching her teeth, and she was stiff with cold. Not to complain had become a matter of honor, almost a reason for survival.

Clouds appeared on the horizon, billowing, burning with light, as if there had been an explosion just beyond their vision. Then hard on their heels came the squall, driving rain turning to sleet, pellets of ice that stung the skin. They bent into it, heads down, and kept going. There was nothing to break the strength of it, nothing to hide behind. They moved carefully, one step at a time.

It cleared again just as suddenly, and they were able to increase speed.

"We need to be in Glen Orchy by night," MacIan said grimly. "There's no place to rest before then, and the Orchy's no river to be stopping near, if ye've no house nor bothy to protect you."

Vespasia did not bother to ask why not; her imagination supplied a dozen answers. She was beginning to feel as if whatever Mrs. Naylor was like, it was going to be a blessed relief to find her and discharge their duty. It could hardly be worse than this. It had assumed nightmare properties. Perhaps the Vikings were right and hell was endless cold, a howling wind, a journey that never arrived anywhere, aching bones and muscles, and always the need to press onward.

Except surely hell could never be so soul-rendingly beautiful?

She saw Isobel sway in the saddle ahead of her, and more than once she was afraid she would fall herself, but by dusk they saw lights ahead of them. It seemed another endless, excruciating hour before they reached them and found them to be the windows of a large house, far greater in size than that for a single family.

Someone must have seen them come, because the door opened wide as their ponies' hooves clattered in the yard, and a large man with a storm-weathered face stood holding a lantern high.

"Well, MacIan, is it you, then? And what are you doing out on a night like this? Who is it you have with you? Ladies, is it? Well, come on inside then. I'll send Andrew and Willie out to tend to your ponies."

"Aye, Finn, it's a dreich night now," MacIan agreed cheerfully, climbing out of the saddle in an easy movement and turning back to help first Isobel and then Vespasia to the ground. Vespasia was horrified to discover she could barely stand up, and but for MacIan's hand, she would have staggered and lost her balance.

The door was held wide, and two young men passed her, nodding shyly on their way to tend to the animals. Inside was blessedly warm. She was dizzy with relief. It was not until she had taken off her wet outer clothes and dried her face on the clean, rough towel handed her that she turned to see the woman standing in the doorway and regarding her with interest. She was tall, easily as tall as Vespasia, with auburn hair wound carelessly on her head, simply as had been convenient. She wore rough wool clothes, quite obviously designed for warmth and convenience of movement. Her face was wide-eyed, intelligent, handsome in a unique and highly individual way. Before she spoke, Vespasia knew that this was Mrs. Naylor.

She turned to Isobel, who seemed frozen, as if now that the moment had come, she could not find the courage. Crossing the moor had cost all she had.

Vespasia stepped forward. "Mrs. Naylor? My name is Vespasia Cumming-Gould." She indicated Isobel. "My friend Isobel Alvie. I apologize for arriving without permission at this hour. We had not realized quite what traveling from

Inverness would involve."

"Beatrice Naylor," the woman answered, a definite smile on her lips. "No one does, the first time. But it is an experience that remains indelibly in the mind. What brings you to the Orchy, in December? It has to be of the utmost importance."

Vespasia turned to Isobel. They had already set foot through the door. Could they accept this woman's hospitality, even on a night like this, at the end of the earth, by answering her question with a lie?

Isobel's face was flushed from the sudden warmth inside, but white around the eyes and lips. The final moment of testing had come, the last and the greatest, upon which all the rest depended.

Vespasia realized she was holding

her breath, her hands clenched at her sides. She could not help. If she did, she would rob Isobel forever of the chance to earn her redemption.

Mrs. Naylor was waiting.

"Yes, it is of the utmost importance," Isobel said at last, her words half-swallowed, her voice trembling. "I have never found anything harder in my life than bringing you the news that your daughter Gwendolen is dead. And I am bitterly ashamed that I contributed to the circumstances which brought it about." She held out the envelope. Traveling had bent it a little, but it remained sealed. "This is the letter she wrote to you."

The man who had opened the door to them moved silently to Mrs. Naylor and put his arm around her, holding her steady. He did it as naturally as if physical contact between them were understood. There was a great tenderness in his face, but he did not speak.

The silence stretched until the pain in it was a tangible thing in the room.

"I see," Mrs. Naylor said at last. "How did it happen?" She stared at Isobel with huge, almost unblinking eyes, as if she could read everything that was in Isobel's mind and beneath it, in the search for a truth she would rather not look at, even herself.

Isobel struggled to tear her gaze away, and failed. "At Applecross," she began, falteringly. "It was a long weekend house party, rather more of a week. I don't know if —"

"I am perfectly acquainted with weekend house parties, Mrs. Alvie," Mrs. Naylor said coldly. "You do not need to explain society or its customs to me. How did my daughter die, and what cause have you to blame yourself? I might think you spoke only as a manner of expressing your sympathy, but I can see in your face that you are in some very real way responsible." She looked briefly at Vespasia. "Does this include you also, Lady Vespasia? Or are you here simply as chaperone?"

Vespasia was startled that Mrs. Naylor knew of her, as the use of her title made clear. "Mrs. Alvie felt the duty to tell you herself, regardless of what the journey involved," she answered. "It is not one a friend would permit her to attempt alone."

"Such loyalty . . . ," Mrs. Naylor murmured. "Or do you share the blame?"

"No, she doesn't," Isobel cut in. "It was I who made the remark. Lady Vespasia had nothing to do with it."

Mrs. Naylor blinked. "The remark?"

Finn made a movement to interrupt, but Mrs. Naylor held up her hand peremptorily. "I will hear this! You know me better than to imagine I will faint or otherwise collapse. Tell me, Mrs. Alvie, how did my daughter die?"

Isobel drew a deep, shivering breath. They were all still standing in the big hallway, relieved only of their outer and wettest clothing. No one had yet eaten a morsel.

"She went out after darkness, when the rest of us had retired, and threw herself from the bridge across the end of the ornamental lake," Isobel answered. "We learned it only the next morning, when it was too late."

Finn grasped Mrs. Naylor by both arms, but she did not stagger or lean back against him. Her face was ashen white. "And in what way were you to blame, Mrs. Alvie?" she asked.

No one in the room moved. There was to be no mercy.

"We all believed that Bertie Rosythe would propose marriage to her that weekend," Isobel said hoarsely, her voice a dry rustle in the silence. "I made a cruel remark to the effect that she would not have loved him, had he been penniless or a servant. I made it from envy, because I also am a widow and had hoped to remarry, possibly to Bertie." She took a deliberate, shuddering breath. "I had no idea it would cause her such distress, but I accept that it did. Apparently he did not go after her to tell her that he knew it was nonsense. I . . . I am deeply ashamed." She did not look away but remained facing Mrs. Naylor.

"You do not need to tell me why you chose that particular barb," Mrs. Naylor said quietly, her voice brittle, every word falling with clarity. "Your face betrays that you heard the rumors and knew the weakness in her armor. Please don't let yourself down by denying it."

The tears stood out in Isobel's eyes. "I wasn't going to," she answered. Vespasia wondered if that were true, and was glad it had not been put to the test. She hated standing here helplessly, but to be of any value, this had to play itself out to the bitter end.

"Who else is aware of this?" Mrs. Naylor asked.

"No one, so far as I am aware," Isobel answered. "Except Lady Vespasia."

Mrs. Naylor turned to Vespasia.

"That is true," Vespasia told her. "Mr. Omegus Jones arranged that she should be buried privately — in the chapel in his grounds, by a minister he knows who would regard it as an accident. If we brought you the news, in person, those others present at Applecross that weekend are bound by oath to say nothing of what happened which would challenge that account."

"Really? And why would they do that?" Mrs. Naylor asked skeptically. "Society loves a scandal. Was it a group of saints you had there?" Her voice was hard-edged with grief and bitter past experience.

"No," Vespasia answered before Isobel could. She moved a fraction forward toward the center of the room, commanding Mrs. Naylor's attention. "They were very ordinary, self-regarding, ambitious, fragile people, just like those it seems you already know. They regarded Mrs. Alvie as to blame and were ready to ruin her, with that certain degree of pleasure that comes when you can do so with an excuse of self-righteousness."

Mrs. Naylor's face twisted at the memory, but she did not interrupt. Vespasia had her complete attention. The rest of the room, Finn, the fire crackling in the hearth, the wind beating against the window need not have existed.

"Mr. Jones proposed a trial, the verdict of which was to bind us, upon our oath," Vespasia went on. "Whoever was found guilty should undertake a journey of expiation, which if completed, would wash out the sin. If they failed, then everyone else was free to ostracize them completely. But if they succeeded, then anyone who referred to it afterwards, for any reason public or private, should themselves meet with that same ostracism."

"How very clever," Mrs. Naylor said softly. "Your Mr. Jones is a man of the greatest wisdom. Expiation? I like that word. It conveys far more than punishment, or even repayment. It is a cleansing. Am I bound by this also?" She turned to Isobel, then back to Vespasia.

"You cannot be," Vespasia answered, seeing the one ghastly flaw in Omegus's plan. "You were not party to the oath." She smiled faintly, like a ghost. "And it does not seem you would be greatly affected if society did not speak to you. I find it difficult to imagine you would know, let alone care."

"You are quite right," Mrs. Naylor agreed. "But this is sufficient explanation for tonight. You have ridden far, and in inclement weather. We have food aplenty and room to spare. And your ponies need rest, whether you do or not." She looked at Isobel. "It will perhaps be harder for you to accept my hospitality than it will be for me to give it, but there is none other for miles around, so you had best learn to do it. Jean will find you rooms and food. I wish to retire and read my daughter's last letter to me." And she took Finn's arm and went out, neither of them turning to look behind.

Isobel and Vespasia had no alternative but to follow Jean, a silent, buxom woman, to where she offered them food and rooms for the night. When they were settled, with the luggage placed conveniently for them, Isobel came to Vespasia's door and accepted instantly the invitation to come in. Her face was pale, her dark eyes shadowed with misery.

"I'd almost rather sleep on the moor!" she said wretchedly. "She knows that! What do you think she'll do tomorrow? Can we leave?"

"No. It is part of our oath that we accompany her to London, if she will allow us to," Vespasia reminded her.

Isobel closed her eyes, her fists clenched by her sides. "I don't think I can! Seven hundred miles, or more, with that woman! That is more punishment than I deserve, Vespasia. I said something stupid, a dozen words, that's all!"

"Cruel," Vespasia reminded her quietly, then wished she had been less blunt. It was not necessary. Isobel was perfectly aware of her fault. Vespasia had no right to demand proof of it every time. "And apart from finishing the task," she said more gently, "I am not at all sure that we can leave here without Mrs. Naylor's assistance. Do you have the faintest idea how to? I don't even know where we are, do you?"

"I must be mad!" Isobel was close

to despair. "You're right. I expect MacIan is on her side, and most certainly Finn is. Who is he, anyway? For that matter, what is this place, and what in the name of heaven is Mrs. Naylor doing here? Apart from apparently living in sin!"

Vespasia ignored the gibe. "I don't know," she said. "But it is an interesting question. Why would a wealthy woman in her middle years choose to spend her time not only a great distance from the rest of society of any sort, but a virtually impossible distance? In fact, why did she not return to London after Kilmuir's death, when Gwendolen did? It would be the most natural thing to do."

"The only answer is that there was an estrangement," Isobel answered. "Perhaps she will not wish to return to London, with us or alone."

"Sleep on the thought, if you wish," Vespasia said dryly. "But do not hold it longer than tomorrow morning." She gave her a smile with as much warmth in it as she could find strength for. "We shall surmise it," she added. "Just think of Lady Warburton's face. She will be fit to spit teeth."

Isobel forced herself to smile back, recognizing kindness, if not practical help, and bade her good night.

Vespasia meant to consider the puzzling question further when she was alone, but the bed was warm and soft, and she sank almost immediately into a nearly dreamless sleep.

When she awoke it was to find Mrs. Naylor herself standing at the foot of the bed with a tray of tea in her hand. She set it on the table and sat down. It was apparent that she had no intention of being dismissed until she was ready to leave. Vespasia might be an earl's daughter, but Mrs. Naylor was on her own territory, and no one could mistake it.

"Thank you," Vespasia said as calmly as she was able to.

"Drink it," Mrs. Naylor responded. "I've had mine." She poured it and passed the cup to Vespasia. "I have read my daughter's letter. I have no intention of telling either you or Mrs. Alvie what was in it, but I should like you to answer a few questions before I accompany you south to pay my respects at the grave."

Vespasia's response would normally have been anger, but there was both a gravity and a pain in this woman that made anything so self-indulgent seem absurd.

"I will tell you what I can," she said instead, sitting upright in the bed and sipping her tea. She should have felt at a disadvantage, dressed as she was in no more than her nightgown and with her hair around her shoulders, but Mrs. Naylor's candor made that irrelevant also.

"What was your real reason for coming here with Mrs. Alvie?" Mrs. Naylor asked.

Vespasia's ready answer died on her lips. This wild place where life and death hung on a pony's footstep, a few inches between the sure path and the cliff edge or the freezing, squelching bog, stripped one of the pretensions that meant so much in society.

"Then I will tell you," Mrs. Naylor answered for her. "You were afraid she would not make it alone, her courage would fail her, and she would take the many excuses to turn back, if not the first, then the second. Why? What does it matter to you if she fails?"

Vespasia thought for only a moment, then she spoke with absolute certainty. "Omegus Jones spoke of a pilgrimage of expiation, in medieval times," she said. "Then it was so dangerous that often the traveler did not return, but it was an act of supreme friendship for a companion to go with them. It seemed right to me to go, perhaps for my own reasons as well as hers." Only as she said the words did she realize their truth. She had her own expiation to make, for Rome, for dreams she should not have allowed herself to entertain, journeys of the heart she should not have made.

"I see," Mrs. Naylor said. "This Mr. Jones seems to be a remarkable man."

"Yes," Vespasia agreed too quickly, and too sincerely.

Mrs. Naylor smiled. "And that also, I think, has something to do with your reason!"

Vespasia found herself blushing, something she had not done in some time. She was accustomed to being in control of herself, if not always of the situation.

"Those of us who have lived any of our passions have something to expiate," Mrs. Naylor said gently. "And those who have nothing are the more to be pitied. My father used to say that if you have never made a mistake, then you have probably never made anything at all. Perhaps Mrs. Alvie will realize that in time also. I shall return with you tomorrow, when the ponies have had time to rest and to eat. I have my own journey to make. We shall follow the High Road south, to Tyndrum, and Crianlarich, to Loch Lomond, and from there to Glasgow where we can find a train to London. It will take several days. How many will depend upon the weather, but we should be at Applecross before Christmas." She stood up. "You may do as you please today, but I would suggest that you do not leave the house. You don't know your way, and the Orchy is a hungry river. It reaches out from its banks and claims many lives."

"Mrs. Naylor?"

She turned. "Yes?"

"What is it in this place that holds you?" It was an impertinent question, yet she wished to know so intensely that she defied all the rules of courtesy to ask.

"It is a place of rest on my own journey, Lady Vespasia. Perhaps after I have bidden farewell to my daughter, it may even prove to be the end of it. Why or how is not your concern." She walked to the door, her back ramrod straight, her head high.

Vespasia did not need to be told that the value of Glen Orchy had much to do with Finn, but she was still turning over in her mind the nature of Mrs. Naylor's journey. They had been speaking of the road to answer for mistakes, a nicer word than *sins,* but it held more than the suggestion of mere error. They both knew they were speaking not merely of judgment, but of morality.

She sat in bed sipping her tea and thinking of Kilmuir's terrible death, and the rumors that Isobel had heard, and the gardener's sudden silence at Muir-of-Ord, and most of all of Gwendolen's face when Isobel had suggested obliquely that she could have been attracted to a footman, had he the social position to offer her.

Was Kilmuir really so desperate for children he would have put Gwendolen away by slandering her so completely that society would accept his act, and then marrying Dolly

Twyford, leaving Gwendolen an outcast, branded a whore?

Her imagination raced! The possi-
bilities were hideous! She thought of
her own children, still little, but one
day they would grow up, marry suit-
ably, one hoped with love. What
would she do if her daughter faced
such ruin of her life? She pictured
Kilmuir out driving in the carriage
with Mrs. Naylor, the horse taking
fright, Kilmuir overbalancing and
falling, his wrists caught in the reins.
The answer was there in her mind.
She would have seized the chance
and pushed him and whipped up the
horses; at least, she would have
thought of it! Whether she would ever
have done it she could not know;
please God, she would never find out.

Was that what had happened? And

Gwendolen had seen it? That was the estrangement between her and her mother. Either she had never realized Kilmuir's plan, or she had refused to believe it. Or perhaps she had willed herself to forget it afterwards, to imagine that somehow he would change his mind, and it would all be all right. He would love her again and deny the rumors. Dolly Twyford would recede into the past. Maybe one day she would even have the longed-for children herself!

And then Mrs. Naylor had ruined it! That would be an estrangement sufficient to send Gwendolen to London, and keep her mother in the farthest reaches of Scotland, farther even than Muir-of-Ord. Perhaps only Glen Orchy would answer that guilt, and maybe even the fear of exposure.

Who else might know? Only the staff of the house where it had happened, and they would keep silence, if not from loyalty, then at least for lack of proof. But Mrs. Naylor would no longer wish to live there.

And if she had not done it, would Kilmuir have gone ahead and first slandered Gwendolen and then cast her aside, destitute, and with no home, no friends, no reputation, no skills to earn her own way, except to sell her body on the streets, or more probably, to take her life — as in the end she had done?

Was that what she had heard in Isobel's remark — a beginning of the old accusation again? Was it history repeating itself, and Bertie Rosythe believing just as Kilmuir had pretended to? That might indeed make her despair and embrace death of her own choosing before ruin should overtake her. There was no mother to defend her this time.

How desperately alone she must have felt — a second time falsely accused, and no denial would help. How can one deny something that has only been hinted at, never said? Some people might have attacked in return, but where would that end? Almost certainly in a defeat even more painful. This way ended it almost before it began, certainly before any but a handful of people knew of it.

And then the worst possibility of all struck her. Had Gwendolen believed that Isobel knew Kilmuir's charge and was very subtly telling her so, and threatening a lifelong blackmail, a cat-and-mouse torture never to end?

If that was true, no wonder she had killed herself! The thought was hideous beyond the mind to realize. Could it even be true? She hated herself that she could even frame the idea — but Isobel's anger, her need came sharply into focus, as if it had been moments ago that Vespasia had seen the look in her eyes, the desperation for her own social position and safety. Then sanity reasserted itself and she thrust it away. It had been a moment's cruelty, no more.

She rose and dressed at last, weighed down by a sadness and an overwhelming pity for both Gwendolen and Mrs. Naylor. She went downstairs to find breakfast; she knew the wisdom of not attempting anything on an empty stomach, however little she felt like eating.

She found Isobel downstairs, pacing the floor. She turned around the moment she heard Vespasia's footsteps. She looked very pale, dark circles around her eyes making her look ill. "Where have you been?" she demanded.

"I slept late," Vespasia answered. "And I did not get up immediately." That was true as far as it went. She had decided not to tell Isobel of her conversation with Mrs. Naylor, and certainly not of the thoughts that had resulted from it. She was ashamed of where it had led her. She liked Isobel, she always had, but perhaps she did not now trust her as deeply as she once had.

"What are we going to do all day?" Isobel pressed. "What is this place, do you suppose? I have seen all sorts of people here, as if it were a religious retreat."

"Perhaps it is." The thought was not absurd. One could hardly retreat further than this!

Vespasia had a breakfast of oatmeal porridge, then toast and very sharp, pungent marmalade, which, when she inquired, she was told was made on the premises. She immediately purchased two jars to take away with her, regardless of the inconvenience of carrying them. One was for herself, the other for Omegus Jones. She knew his tastes; she had watched him at his own table.

They spent the day quietly. The house proved indeed to be a form of retreat, not religious, but beyond question spiritual. Mrs. Naylor had found a vocation in listening to the troubled, the lonely, and the guilty whose fears robbed them of courage, or the hope that battles could be won.

Vespasia found herself wishing they might stay longer, and she forced herself to remember that this was not her calling, certainly not now, when winter was closing in rapidly. They must accompany Mrs. Naylor to London, and then return to Apple-cross to report to Omegus and to face Lady Warburton and the others, if they were to still their tongues before spring. They would be bound by the silence of expectation only so long.

She saw Finn several times and observed in him a humor and a great strength of self-understanding, and she perceived without effort why Mrs. Naylor found happiness with him. There was a reserve in him so that there would always be thoughts and dreams to surprise.

It was with regret that she and Isobel set out at daybreak the following morning, with Mrs. Naylor and MacIan, and a troop of ponies. Finn saw them to the entrance of the yard, standing with the fierce wind blowing his hair and whipping at his coat. Vespasia knew his good-byes to Mrs. Naylor had already been said, and words were an encumbrance to the understanding they shared.

They set off south, away from the Glen along the High Road. It was almost seven miles to Tyndrum, and another five or so to Crianlarich. If they pressed on with only such breaks as the horses needed, they might make it by nightfall. On easy roads a carriage would have done it by luncheon, but this was wild country, the peaks snow-covered. They went in the teeth of a gale with ice on its edge, and one good blizzard might end their journey altogether.

But Mrs. Naylor did not hesitate. She led the way with MacIan and left Vespasia and Isobel to keep up the best they could. Their ponies were as good as anyone's; it was a matter of human endurance, and they were half her age. If Mrs. Naylor even thought of doubting them, she gave no sign of it.

They plodded silently through a great sweeping wilderness of mountain and sky, sometimes lit by dazzling sun, blinding off the snow slopes above and ahead. Then squalls would drive down from nowhere, and they huddled together, backs to the worst of it, until it was past and they would plow forward again.

Vespasia glanced at Isobel and received a rueful smile in answer. It was as clear as if they had spoken; At least this flesh-withering cold, the slow, uneven progress, the need to guide their ponies with all possible attention, and even the waste of time to get off and walk, knee-deep in fresh snow, skirts sodden to the thighs, made conversation completely impossible. With Gwendolen's death heavy on heart and mind, it was a blessing, however profound the disguise.

It was well past midday when they reached the inn at Tyndrum, and the weather was closing in as if it would be all but dark by three.

"We'll no make Crianlarich the

night," MacIan said, squinting upward at the sky. "It's after one now, an' it's another five hard miles. We'd best rest the ponies an' start fresh in the morning."

"Surely we can make five miles by dark?" Isobel said urgently. "We've done most of it already!"

"We've done seven, Mistress Alvie," MacIan told her dourly. "Ye mebbe think ye can do the like again, in two hours, but ye're mistaken. An' I'll no have ye drive my ponies to it. Rest while ye can, and be glad of a spot o' warmth." He looked at Mrs. Naylor. "Take a dram, mistress. I'll care for the beasts. Get ye inside."

It was what Vespasia also had dreaded, a long afternoon by the fireside with Isobel and Mrs. Naylor. The meal was endurable. They were all still numb with cold and glad of any food at all, let alone hot, savory haggis rich with herbs, offered them in spite of the nearness to Burns's night. It was served with mashed potatoes and sweet turnips, and afterwards flat, unleavened oatcakes and a delicately flavored cheese covered with oatmeal, called Cabac.

It was finally cleared away, and they were left alone in the small sitting room by the fire, peat to replenish it on the hearth, stags' heads on the wall. The silence was leaden, and Vespasia saw the slight smile cross Mrs. Naylor's lips. She knew in that instant that Mrs. Naylor understood exactly what was in Isobel's mind, and Vespasia's, and that she was mistress of herself sufficiently to outlast both of them. Grief would wound her, perhaps to the heart, but it would not bend or break her. She would meet them on her own terms.

Twice Isobel began to speak, and then stopped. Finally Mrs. Naylor turned to her.

"Is there something you wish to say, Mrs. Alvie?"

Isobel shook her head. "Only that we cannot sit here in silence all afternoon, but I see that we can, if that is what you wish."

"What would you like to speak about?"

Isobel had no answer.

"Glen Orchy," Vespasia said suddenly. "I should like to know about how you found it, and how word travels of what you do there, and who is welcome."

Mrs. Naylor regarded her with a

wry humor, the smile all turned inward, as if facing some moment of decision at last. "You do not ask what I do there, or why I stay," she observed. "Is that because you believe I would not tell you? Or does courtesy suggest it would be intrusive?"

"Both," Vespasia replied. "But principally because I believe that I know."

Isobel looked confused.

Mrs. Naylor ignored her. "Do you indeed?" she said dubiously. "I think not, but we shall not discuss it. If there is debt between us, and I am not sure that there is, then it is you who owe me."

"I have children," Vespasia said gently. She was going to add that she knew the consuming love and need to protect, then she saw the warning in

Mrs. Naylor's face, the sudden tight-
ening of fear, and she remembered
also that Isobel had been widowed
before she had had a chance to bear
children. So she said nothing, but she
knew that she was right, and Mrs.
Naylor knew it also. For the first
time, Vespasia took charge of the
conversation. She repeated her questions. Mrs. Naylor answered them,
and through the darkening afternoon
both younger women heard a story of
extraordinary courage and strength
of will, compassion, and determina-
tion, but told in a way that made it
seem the most natural and ordinary
thing, in fact the only possible way to
behave.

Out of an empty house falling into
dereliction, Mrs. Naylor and Finn
had built and repaired it, until the

house was restored to its earlier comfort. Then one guest at a time, first by chance, it had become a hostelry for wanderers who needed shelter not only from the elements of the Highland winter, but from the harder seasons of life, a time to rest and regain not so much strength as a sense of direction, an understanding of mountains, of paths, and above all of hope.

When they retired after dinner Isobel followed Vespasia up the stairs, almost on her heels. "What am I going to do?" she said when they reached the bedroom they were to share. There was a note of desperation in her voice.

"What you have told Omegus that you will do," Vespasia answered. "Mrs. Naylor won't tell people anything other than whatever you tell them yourself."

"I don't mean about Gwendolen's death!" Isobel said impatiently. "I mean about anything! I don't want to marry Bertie Rosythe, even if he offered! Or anyone like him. I should die of loneliness, even if it took me all my life to do it, an inch a day." Her voice was suddenly harsher, as if the anger ran out of control. "For heaven's sake, are you really so damnably complacent that you don't even know what I mean? Can't you see anything further than money and fashion, the season, knowing everyone who matters and having them know you, going to all the right parties?" She flung her hand out stiffly. "When the door is closed, and you take off your tiara and the maid hangs up your gown? Who are you then?" Now she was almost weeping. "What have you? Have you anything at all that matters? Is that what comfort has given you — that you are dead at heart — of self-satisfaction?"

Vespasia saw the contempt in Isobel's eyes and knew that it had been there dormant for all the time they had known each other. Did she care enough to strip away the armor of her own protection to answer truthfully? If not, then she was denying herself, almost as if she were making it true.

"I have too much pain and too much hope to be dead," she replied gravely. "My best days were not wearing a tiara, or a ball gown. I carried bandages, and water, and sometimes even a gun. I wore a plain gray dress that was borrowed, and I stood on the barricades in Rome, and fought for a revolution that failed." She lowered her voice because the tears choked in her throat. "And loved a man I shall never see again. You have no right to despise anyone, Isobel, until at least you know who they are. And we will probably none of us ever know anyone sufficiently well for that. Be happy for it. It is not a sweet thing to look down on others, or to feel their inferiority. It's lonely, ugly, and wrong. Sleep well. We must make Crianlarich, at least, by to-morrow evening. I know it's only about five miles, but five miles of storm in these hills may seem more than thirty miles at home. Good night."

"Good night," Isobel said gently.

The following day they traveled through glancing blizzards, one of them heavy enough to halt them for over two hours, but they reached Crianlarich before sundown, and the day after as far as the head of Loch Lomond, with Ben Lomond towering white in the distance to the south. After that, they kept close to the water until they were past the Ben itself, and on the morning of the fifth day since leaving Glen Orchy, they bade MacIan good-bye and thanked him heartily. They took the boat to the farthest shore of the loch little more than twenty miles from Glasgow itself. From there it was a matter of hiring a vehicle of any sort and driving their own way to the railway station. With a trap and good roads, even if the weather was inclement, it was a journey that could be done in one day.

After breakfast Isobel was assisted in, then Vespasia, leaving Mrs. Naylor last. Vespasia had intended it so, knowing that Mrs. Naylor was an excellent horsewoman, used to driving. After all, it was she who had gained control of the runaway horse that had killed Kilmuir. Whether it was an accident or not she did not know, nor did she wish to. She herself was a fine rider, but very indifferent at managing a carriage horse, which was a different skill entirely.

Mrs. Naylor hesitated.

Vespasia wondered if memories of Kilmuir's death were returning to her; doubt, guilt, horror, regret — even fear that Gwendolen, having witnessed it from her horse, even a hundred yards away or more, had made her courage for life so fragile. Did she know that her mother had killed to save her? Was that the burden Gwendolen finally could not bear?

Mrs. Naylor sat in the driving seat and picked up the reins awkwardly. She held them in her hands together, not apart in order to give her control of the animal.

The hostler showed her how, patiently, and still she looked clumsy. The horse sensed it and shifted, shaking its head.

The truth struck Vespasia like a hammerblow. Mrs. Naylor did not know how to drive. It was not she who had held the reins when Kilmuir had fallen, accidentally or otherwise; it was Gwendolen herself! Vespasia had seen her in London; she was brilliant at it! And it was Mrs. Naylor who had been out riding and had seen. It made infinitely more sense! She had had to protect her daughter, and Gwendolen, in the shock of it, had allowed herself to forget — to move the blame to a more bearable place.

It fell in front of her eyes in a perfect pattern: The guilt was for having arranged and permitted a marriage to someone like Kilmuir, not to have judged him more accurately. It was a mother's primary duty toward her daughter, and Mrs. Naylor had signally failed. That was why she was prepared to take the burden of guilt now. And Gwendolen had allowed it.

Then in one trivial, cruel remark Gwendolen's fragile new image had been shattered, hope, the shield of forgetting, all gone, and the specter of a lifetime's blackmail from others who knew, or guessed at least part of it.

"I'll drive!" Vespasia said aloud, her voice surprisingly steady. The slight tremor in it could be attributed to the cold. "Let me. I am not as good as Gwendolen was, but I am perfectly adequate." She scrambled forward to take Mrs. Naylor's place. Their eyes met for a moment, and Mrs. Naylor knew that she understood.

Vespasia smiled. It would never be referred to again. Isobel could not afford to — she had her own secrets to keep — and Vespasia had no wish to.

Mrs. Naylor handed her the reins, and they began the last part of their journey to Glasgow, before the long train ride to London.

The journey was tedious, as it had been on the way up, but they reached London at last. It was three days before Christmas. The final meeting was to be at Applecross, and Vespasia knew that Omegus Jones would already be there. There seemed little point in remaining in the city, so she invited Mrs. Naylor and Isobel to go with her to her own country house, which was within ten miles of Applecross. She was uncertain if Mrs. Naylor would wish to accept, and was surprised how it pleased her when she did.

Part Three

After greeting her husband and children, the first thing Vespasia did was to write a letter to Omegus Jones and tell him that they had completed their mission, and it remained only to report that fact to make the oath binding. Then she sealed it and called one of the footmen to ride over and deliver it.

"Shall I wait for an answer, my lady?" he asked.

"Oh, yes! Yes, indeed," she answered him. "It is of the utmost importance!"

"Yes, my lady."

When he returned several hours later and gave her the envelope, she thanked him and tore it open without waiting for him to leave.

My dear Vespasia,

You cannot know how relieved I am to hear that you are safely returned, and that you have accomplished in full all you set out to do. The letter of the law would have sufficed to bind our fellows to silence, but it is the spirit which heals the transgressor, and that is in essence what matters.

I admit I have worried about you, veering from one moment having the utmost faith that you would come to no harm, and the next being plunged into an abyss of fear that some natural disaster might overtake you. Had I known the true extent of your journey to the north, I should not have allowed you to go, and none of this would have succeeded. Perhaps it is good that at times we do not know what lies ahead, or we would not attempt it, and failure would be inevitable.

Naturally, you will wish to be with your own family for Christmas Day, but will you bring Isobel and Mrs. Naylor to Applecross on Christmas Eve, so we may complete our covenant, and Isobel be free?

I await your answer with hope,
                    Your friend and servant,
                    Omegus Jones

She folded it with a smile and placed it in her escritoire in the drawer that had a lock on it, then she found Isobel and Mrs. Naylor and gave them Omegus's invitation. The following morning she sent the same footman back with their acceptance.

They set out in the afternoon in order to arrive at Applecross for dinner. The day was crisp and cold, but this far south there was no snow yet, only a taste of frost in the air. By the time they arrived they were shivering, even beneath traveling rugs, and glad to alight and go into the great hall decked with holly and ivy, scarlet ribbons, gold-tipped pine-cones, and great bowls of fruit. The fire blazed in the hearth, burning half a log. Footmen met them with glasses of mulled wine and marzipan sweet-meats, warm mince pies and candied peel.

In the hall was a huge fir tree decked with ornaments, candles, and chains of bright-colored paper. Beneath it were small, gaily wrapped gifts. The tree's woody aroma filled the air, along with wood smoke, spiced scents, and, very faintly, the promise of roasted Christmas dinner and hot plum pudding. There was excitement in the whisper of maids' voices and the quick rustle of their skirts.

Omegus was delighted to see them. He complimented Isobel, offered his deepest sympathies to Mrs. Naylor, and said he would tell her all she wished to know when she felt ready to ask, and would take her to the grave at her convenience.

She thanked him and said that festivities of the season must come first. It was a brave and generous thing to do, and exactly what Vespasia would have expected of her.

Ten minutes later when the others had gone, Omegus took Vespasia's arm and held her with a startlingly firm grip when she made to move away. "I think you have more to tell me," he said quietly.

She swiveled to face him. "More?"

He smiled very slightly. "I know you, my dear," he told her. "You would not like Mrs. Naylor, as I see you obviously do, unless you had come to know her more than superficially. You have learned something of her which has moved you to admiration, something you do not give lightly. The same emotion is not in Isobel, so it seems likely to me that you have not confided it in her. I wonder why not, and the answer is possibly to do with Gwendolen's death. Is it something I should know?"

Vespasia found herself blushing. She had not intended to tell him, and now she found she could not lie. It was not that she had not the imagination — it would have been simple enough — but she would lose something she valued intensely were she to place that barrier between them.

In a low, very soft voice, she told him what she had guessed and deduced of the truth of Kilmuir's death.

"And you did not tell Isobel?" he asked gravely.

"No. It . . ." She saw in his eyes the criticism that was unspoken inside herself. "She has a right to know — doesn't she?" she finished.

"Yes." There was no equivocation in him.

"I shall tell her after dinner," she promised. "After she has made peace with Lady Warburton."

His eyebrows rose in question. "Do you not trust her to keep the same silence for others that she wishes kept for herself?"

Again Vespasia felt the heat burn up her cheeks. "I'm not sure," she confessed. "Mrs. Naylor deserves that silence, and Gwendolen needs it. There is no oath to bind her for that."

He put his hand over hers for an instant, then offered her his arm.

"Shall we go in to dinner?"

The meal was rich and excellent. After the main courses were finished, and long before anyone could think of the ladies withdrawing, Omegus rose to his feet, and the talk ceased.

"My friends, we are met together this Christmas Eve in order to keep an oath that we made less than a month ago. We promised then that if Isobel Alvie were to travel to Scotland and find Gwendolen's mother, Mrs. Naylor, and give her Gwendolen's last letter, and should Mrs. Naylor be willing, accompany her back here, then we would wipe from our memory all knowledge of her remarks to Gwendolen on the night of her death. Her part of that oath has been fulfilled."

"You expect us to take her word for that?" Fenton Twyford asked, his face twisted in sarcasm.

"Mrs. Naylor is here," Omegus answered him. "If you have doubts of Isobel, or of me, then you may ask her." He indicated Mrs. Naylor where she sat calm and dignified at the table.

Fenton Twyford turned to her, met an icy stare, and changed his mind. Then he became aware of his impertinence and blushed.

The flicker of a smile crossed Omegus's face. "It is now up to us to keep our part. Any man or woman who breaks it will cease to be known by the rest of us. We will not speak to them again, invite them to any event public or private, or in any way acknowledge their presence. They will have chosen to be a person whose honor is worthless. I cannot imagine anyone wishes to be such a . . . a creature. Mrs. Naylor has promised to be bound by the same code." He turned to her.

"I have," she said clearly. "And I

wish to add to that what Mr. Jones does not know. Mrs. Alvie's part in my daughter's death was smaller than you or she are aware. It was simply the last straw added to a weight Gwendolen was already bearing, placed there by others, of which Mrs. Alvie had only a slight knowledge. I have no intention of telling you what burdens those were. It is better buried with her. Sufficient to say that it would be unjust for Mrs. Alvie to suffer more blame than she has — and which she has washed away by her acts toward me. It is over."

Isobel turned to her, her eyes wide, her lips parted in astonishment and dawning anger. "You mean they were going to punish me — and I was only partly guilty?"

"Yes," Mrs. Naylor agreed.

Isobel swung around to stare at Lady Warburton. "You would have ruined me, driven me into a wilderness from which I would never recover! And I wasn't even guilty! Not entirely . . ."

Lady Warburton quaked. "I didn't know!" she protested. "I thought you were!"

"You thought so yourself!" Blanche Twyford added. "You didn't deny it!"

"Yes, I did!" Isobel spat at her. "You gave no mercy!"

"That is true," Omegus cut across her, his voice clear and insistent, undeniable. "And mercy, the gift to forgive, to wash away from the memory as if it had not happened, to accept the gift of God which is love and hope, courage to begin again in the faith that redemption is come into the world, is the meaning of Christmas. That is why we are met here today. It is why we deck the halls with holly, why the bells will ring tonight from village to village across the land until the earth and the sky are filled with their sound." He turned to Isobel, waiting for her answer, not in words on her lips, but in her eyes.

She hesitated only a moment. "Of course," she answered softly. "I have made my journey and arrived at Christmas, perhaps only at this moment. I shall be grateful all my life that you offered it to me, and to Vespasia for coming with me, when she had no need. How could I accept it for myself, and deny it to another?"

"It is everyone's journey," Omegus said with a smile of utter sweetness.

"No man needs to make it alone. But his choice to go with another is the one act of friendship which brings us closest to the Man who was born on the first Christmas, and is the Gift of them all." He raised his glass. "To the friendship which never fades!"

All around the table the answering glasses were lifted.

About the Author

Anne Perry is the bestselling author of *No Graves as Yet: A Novel of World War I*, as well as two acclaimed series set in Victorian England. Her William Monk novels include *Death of a Stranger*, *Funeral in Blue*, *Slaves of Obsession*, and *The Twisted Root*. She also writes the popular novels featuring Thomas and Charlotte Pitt, including *Seven Dials*, *Southampton Row*, *The Whitechapel Conspiracy*, and *Half Moon Street*. Her short story "Heroes" won an Edgar Award. Anne Perry lives in Scotland. Visit her Web site at www.anneperry.net.

The employees of Thorndike Press hope you have enjoyed this Large Print book. All our Thorndike and Wheeler Large Print titles are designed for easy reading, and all our books are made to last. Other Thorndike Press Large Print books are available at your library, through selected bookstores, or directly from us.

For information about titles, please call:

(800) 223-1244

or visit our Web site at:

www.gale.com/thorndike
www.gale.com/wheeler

To share your comments, please write:

Publisher
Thorndike Press
295 Kennedy Memorial Drive
Waterville, ME   04901